PADDOCK GROVE

This is a work of fiction. Names, characters, places and incidents are either the product of the author's imagination or, if real, used fictitiously. All statements, activities, stunts, descriptions, information and material of any other kind contained herein are included for entertainment purposes only and should not be relied on for accuracy or replicated as they may result in injury.

First published 2025 by Walker Books Ltd
87 Vauxhall Walk, London SE11 5HJ

2 4 6 8 10 9 7 5 3 1

EU Authorized Representative: HackettFlynn Ltd, 36 Cloch Choirneal, Balrothery, Co. Dublin, K32 C942, Ireland. EU@walkerpublishinggroup.com

This book has been typeset in Adobe Garamond Pro

Printed and bound by CPI Group (UK) Ltd, Croydon CR0 4YY

British Library Cataloguing in Publication Data:
a catalogue record for this book is available from the British Library

ISBN 978-1-5295-2284-6

www.walker.co.uk

PADDOCK GROVE

A Pony to Own

J. P. ROSE

WALKER BOOKS

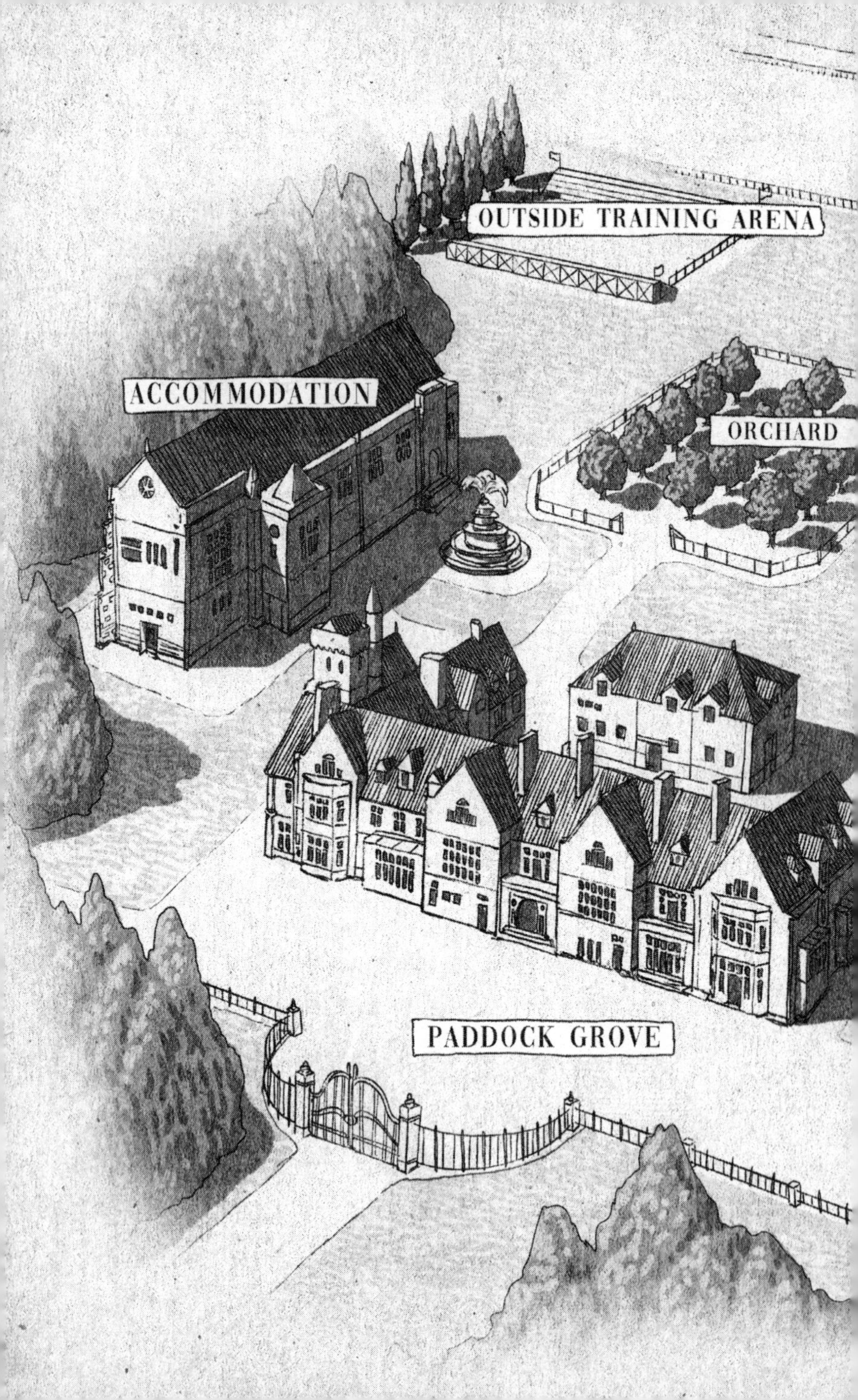
OUTSIDE TRAINING ARENA
ACCOMMODATION
ORCHARD
PADDOCK GROVE

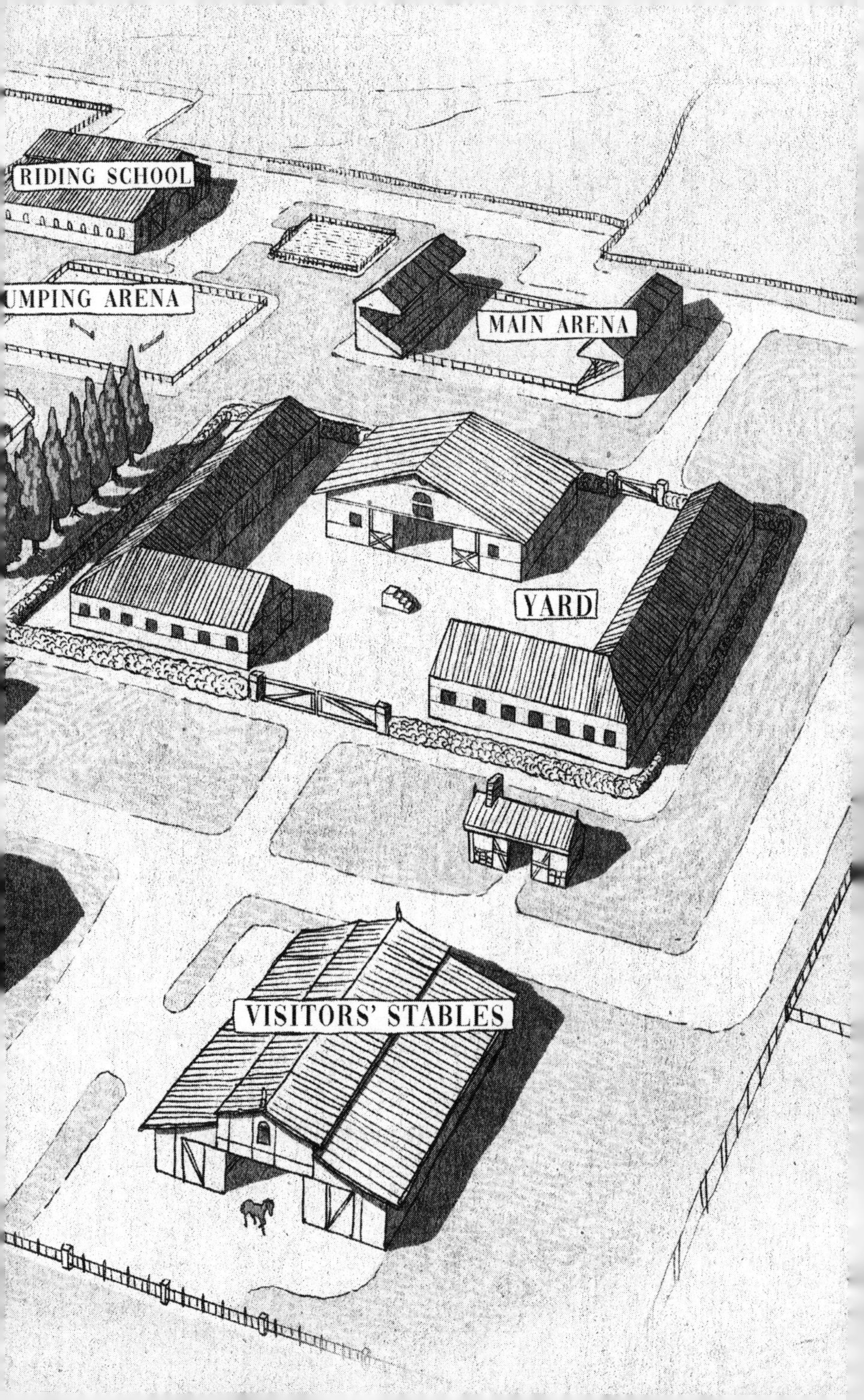
RIDING SCHOOL
UMPING ARENA
MAIN ARENA
YARD
VISITORS' STABLES

LIST OF CHARACTERS

Georgia 'George' Harris – A talented young rider starting at Paddock Grove. Keen to prove that she deserves her place among her classmates.

Bear – A scruffy, mischievous piebald cob from George's riding school with a big appetite and a mind of his own. (Especially good at undoing knots, gates and stable doors.)

STROLLER HOUSE

Katie Ellis – Sensible and kind-hearted. Katie takes school very seriously, sometimes a little too seriously. She hates to let people down.

Sheriff – A homebred light bay gelding that Katie helped train from a foal. Has a strong, trusting bond with Katie.

Lili Nagata – Light-hearted Lili is fun to be around but sometimes struggles to take things seriously. She's a chatterbox, except when it comes to the secret she holds.

Ted – Lili's horse, a beautiful warmblood whose show-ring name is Lord Moonbeam but goes by his stable name, Ted. Excellent in the arena but doesn't like cross-country.

Tabitha Bailey – Can be stand-offish and strong-willed. Sometimes she comes across as insensitive. Loans her horse from the school.

Misty Dumas – A student from France who is skilled in dressage. Straight and honest.

Dream – Highly trained palomino belonging to Misty.

OTHER STUDENTS

Meg Lopez – A student who likes to get her own way. From rival Frankel House.

Jessica Travis – Unfriendly and snooty. Also in Frankel House.

Harriet Chambers – A mean girl who thinks she's better than everyone else.

SCHOOL STAFF

Mrs Hawksworth – Headmistress

Ms Stopcroft – Head riding coach

Miss Fox – School veterinarian

Mr Thatcher – Yard manager

Mrs Winters – Housemistress for Stroller House

Mr Bassey – School bursar

Chapter One

THE MESSY SURPRISE

Had Georgia Harris known what the day was going to bring, she might well have gone back to bed. As it was, she found herself standing under the September sky, outside a dilapidated sheep shed on the farm behind her house.

Georgia wasn't actually *sure* what she was supposed to be looking at. Nor was she sure why her mum and dad, along with old farmer Albert, their eighty-year-old neighbour, were standing grinning at her. *Everyone* including her friends had been acting rather strangely towards her lately, come to think of it. Even Mrs Crawley, who worked at the village post office and usually stopped to have a friendly chat, had hurried past Georgia when she'd seen her yesterday.

The other curious thing about the past few days was that her parents had been doing a lot of whispering. Each time Georgia had entered the room, they'd quickly stopped talking and mysteriously started "doing something". So far this week she'd caught her mum loading the washing machine with her clean, ironed jumpers. Then she'd caught her dad tying his shoelaces on a pair of slip-on shoes. It had all been very odd.

"Your dad and I have been bursting to tell you, George." Buzzing with excitement, George's mum was hopping up and down on the spot as though she was trying to keep warm, causing her long, wavy, mousy-brown hair to tumble out of the bun tied loosely on the top of her head. "But we wanted it to be a surprise... We all did."

Albert, whose face was drawn with deep lines, wiped his hand over his stubbly chin. He squinted at George, then nodded to the large sheep shed with its battered old wooden door. "Go on then, lass, open it up."

George glanced between them all. Her dad broke into a smile. His crown of thick, jet-black dreadlocks swung forward as he gave her a brief, tight hug, and when he stepped back the bright afternoon made his smooth ebony skin shine almost as much as his eyes. "We're so proud of you, George. If anyone deserves this, you do. We know that you've wanted this for so long."

George's stomach knotted as she looked at the wooden door, and her heart skipped a beat. From as far back as she could remember, the only thing George had dreamt of was a horse of her own. Now that the riding school she'd attended since she was four years old had been forced to close down and sell off the horses, she'd thought maybe ... possibly ... well, her dream would come true, especially now she'd won a scholarship to the Paddock Grove equine boarding school. Her mind suddenly flooded with thoughts of Timmy – the horse she'd bonded with, her soulmate... Could it be? Could it *really* be her beloved Timmy, who had belonged to the local riding school and she'd been *desperate* to own?

"Don't keep us waiting, your mum looks like she's going to burst!" Her dad laughed again, and George could feel their excitement crackling in the air.

She slowly walked towards the shed. With trembling hands, she pulled the stiff, rusty bolt across. After a brief glance over her shoulder to her parents and Albert, who all nodded reassuringly, she took a deep breath and…

"Timmy! Timmy!" George excitedly called out his name as she opened the door. "Tim—" But the rest of his name caught in the back of her throat as a white face with unfamiliar dark eyes stared at her. George's mouth dropped open as she stared back.

Instead of Timmy's sleek form, George saw a scruffy piebald cob with a thick mane and a messy coat covered in soaked oats. There were grass stains on his white patches and he had long, tangled feathers that covered his hooves.

"Meet Bear." George's dad walked up behind her. He wrapped his arm round her shoulders.

"B–B–Bear?" George blinked, then blinked some more, trying to stop her heart sinking. *Bear?!* Oh *no*!

Bear was also from the local riding school. In fact, she'd often mucked him out when she helped out on Saturdays and any evening during the week when she had no homework, in exchange for riding lessons.

Bear was a cheeky pony known for his huge appetite and mischievous behaviour. Whenever a rider saw that they were scheduled to take Bear for a lesson there was a loud groan. Bear was more interested in eating than doing anything else. More often than not, those riders came back to the stables red-faced and very frustrated with Bear, who wouldn't listen to any sort of instructions. Depending on his mood, he was either a very slow plod or bolted off to get to the nearest patch of grass.

George swallowed hard as she stared at Bear's matted, black tail, which had mud stuck to the bottom of it. "Where's… Where's Timmy?" She hoped she didn't sound rude, but this was a disaster!

"I'm afraid we couldn't afford Timmy, sweetheart. He's gone to another home. They wanted you to have him, but someone else came in with a very high offer, and they had to sell him to the highest bidder." Her mum's voice was tinged with regret, but it was clear she didn't understand. Not really.

"But we thought you'd love Bear just as much," her dad chimed in, looking at George hopefully.

George glanced back at Bear, who was standing by some upturned buckets, busy tucking into a mouthful of sweet-smelling haylage. Bear, like so many cobs, was on the round side, and George's heart sank. She didn't want to be ungrateful, she really didn't, but *look at* him. Bear was everything Timmy wasn't.

Timmy's chestnut coat had gleamed. He was elegant and athletic, highly trained, and glided over huge jumps with ease. He was a dream. A beautiful, shining, well-groomed dream. Bear, however, looked like he'd never seen a grooming brush in his life. Even his white fetlocks were brown with thick clumps of mud. And if that wasn't bad enough, George thought, the highest she'd ever seen Bear jump was the small hedge by the far field when he was being led back to his stable and he pulled away to get to the tractor loaded with bales of meadow hay. Timmy had been her everything since she'd fallen in love with him on the first day he'd arrived at the stables. George might not have owned him, but in her heart it felt like she did. She wanted to cry.

"We know how much you adored Timmy, George," her mum said. "And we know it'll be difficult without him after all this time, but your dad and I are sure you'll have lots of fun with Bear."

The smell of haylage – like ripened bananas – filled

the air as George battled her tears. Timmy, her beloved gelding, had been her best friend for the past two and a half years. She had kissed his soft, velvety nose and fed him three carrots the last time she saw him, crying quietly into his coat – but she hadn't really *believed* that was the last time. So, the thought of not seeing Timmy or riding him ever again made George feel like he'd taken a part of her heart with him to his new home.

Timmy had been her wings. He'd taken her from local pony club events to competing – and earning a spot in – some of the national showjumping competitions. Even when she'd looked at towering jumps on the cross-country courses or in the ring and hadn't felt brave, George had known that the moment she sat in the saddle, Timmy would look after her and never let her down.

"You do like Bear, don't you, George?" Her dad's eyebrows snapped together in a line of worry.

George nodded furiously, wanting to reassure him. Her parents didn't know much about horses, but they'd always supported her, taking her to lessons and competitions in all weathers and cheering her on. She also knew that her parents would've had to work *extra* hard to give her this opportunity of having a pony of her very own. It all made sense now why her dad's recent mission had been to sell off their old things in the loft – and some of the newer things too – as well as all the overtime her mum had taken on at her office job. And, therefore, George certainly didn't want to show them how heartbroken she truly was.

"I–I…" She crossed her fingers behind her back and nodded again. "Yes. Yes… I mean, look at him, Dad, he's … he's … Well, he's…" George paused and scrambled for the right words. She held back tears, desperately trying to hold the smile on her face. She didn't usually tell lies, but on this occasion she thought it was probably best to do so.

Yet again she stared at Bear, who was looking at her through his messy long forelock, as curious as her mum and dad and Albert as they waited for her to finish her sentence. "He's … he's … *beautiful*. That's what he is… He's beautiful, Dad – and Mum – thank you *so much*."

A loud sigh of relief was let out by everyone, and to George it even felt as if the shed itself was breathing out a relieved sigh that she'd found the right words.

“That’s what we all thought. We thought he was beautiful too,” her dad said, beaming. “And Albert’s even found some old tack you can have. He’s sorted out a bridle and saddle.”

As if that was his cue, Albert disappeared into another of his outbuildings.

A minute later, he reappeared carrying a large, heavy-looking brown saddle over his arm and a worn leather bridle.

“It’s old, but it fits him lovely,” Albert said, looking like he was struggling under the weight of it. “And like I’ve always said, a golden bit does nothing to make a horse any better.” George thought it was just as well, since the snaffle hanging from the cheek band was stained the kind of green that would only come off with a fierce scrubbing.

“We’re so excited for you, George.” Her mum warmly laughed out her words.

George threw her arms around her mum and dad, hugging them both tightly, hiding the tear rolling down her face as her heart ached for Timmy.

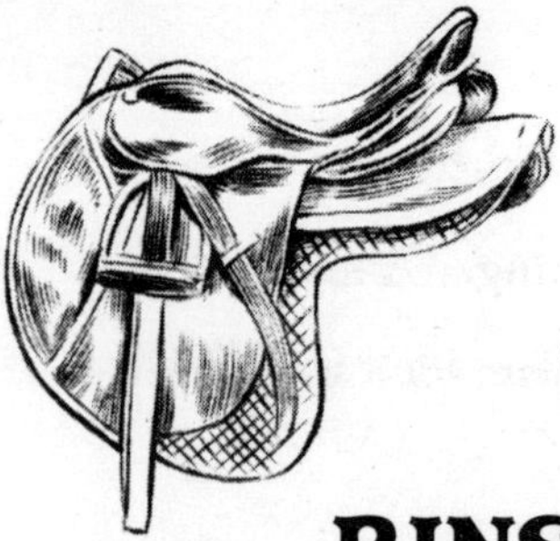

Chapter Two

RINSE AND RUN

"Come on then, get him out," George's dad, who was allergic to horses, encouraged her from a distance. "Then I can take some photos of you both to send to the rest of the family. They were all excited to hear about Bear when Mum told them."

George inwardly groaned. She felt terrible, not just because of Bear, but because she could see how happy her parents were. She hoped they'd never guess that her heart was breaking.

"Oh, I forgot. We also got you this." Her mum reached inside the bag she was carrying on her arm and brought out a small parcel, wrapped in bright red-and-yellow paper.

George took it gratefully. "Thank you." She smiled

and quickly tore open the package. Inside was a beautiful red lead rope, along with a matching red-and-yellow head collar with a small brass nameplate on the side that read: *BEAR*.

"He's a fine lad. Legs in each corner." Farmer Albert gently tapped Bear on his rounded backside, which was strong and powerful. "I reckon he'd be good for pulling a cart, this one."

If George had thought her heart couldn't sink any further, it did then. Everyone was being so kind, but she'd never dreamt, never *wanted*, to own a pony that could pull a cart. The kind of ponies George dreamt of could soar over the jumps, glide across the cross-country course, and dance on air in the dressage ring. Even with all the training in the world, she couldn't imagine that Bear could do anything other than eat hay and plod around the bridleways. Or, as Albert said, pull a cart.

"We also got you this." Her dad handed her a brightly wrapped package that he'd hidden in the corner underneath a pile of clean straw.

George unwrapped it to reveal a brand-new purple

kit box that had her name inscribed on the front in fancy writing. Inside, the brushes were brightly coloured in pinks, blues and yellows. The kit included everything from a dandy brush to a mane comb, a hoof pick and even a bottle of strawberry-scented horse shampoo. Despite her initial disappointment over Bear, George was delighted. "This is brilliant, thank you."

While Albert cheerfully listed all the farm chores Bear could do, as if describing a four-legged tractor instead of a pony, George quietly slipped the head collar over Bear's soft muzzle before gliding it over his ear and fastening the buckle on the side of it. Carefully, she ran her fingers under the cheek strap, making sure it wasn't too tight, then she clipped the lead rope on the ring under his chin before leading Bear out of the sheep shed.

Outside in the late afternoon sun, Bear didn't look any better. In fact, George realized with dismay, he looked even scruffier now she could see him properly! His shaggy coat caught the light, highlighting every single unkempt patch and tangle.

"He'll be perfect to take to Paddock Grove." Her

mum stroked Bear's cheek, which he seemed to like, as the moment she stopped he nudged her with his head to continue.

Paddock Grove? In the whirl of surprise, George had (somehow, incredibly) forgotten about that. She stared at her mum in disbelief. There was no way that Bear could possibly fit in. No way at all. The school was known internationally for its elite equestrian programme. How could she take a cart horse like Bear there?

"Stand next to him, George, and give me a big smile… That's it," George's dad happily instructed her as he started taking photos on his phone. But all George could think of was having to take Bear with her to her new school. The thought made her feel positively ill. "Smile, George."

Going to her new school, she'd wanted everything to be perfect, but taking Bear was far from that. She'd never imagined someone like *her* could get into an amazing place like Paddock Grove – not after missing out last year when she was moving up into Year Seven. She'd been one mark short of passing because she hadn't known any Latin. Actually, she hadn't even known that

Latin was a subject! But her parents had encouraged her to try again for this year's intake.

Mrs Llewellyn, a retired schoolteacher who lived in the village and was skilled in Latin, had helped her, and George had studied very hard for the entrance exam and practised her riding every chance she could. When it had been time to take the riding test at Paddock Grove, the local stables had even let George take Timmy with her.

Despite her nerves, Timmy had been her lucky charm. He'd known exactly what to do. As always, he gave her confidence, making the cross-country course feel effortless. He'd shone in their dressage test too and tackled the school's showjumping ring – including the tricky triple bar and oxer – without breaking a sweat. It'd been the best day *ever,* but she hadn't really imagined she'd get in.

As soon as the acceptance letter arrived, offering her a coveted full scholarship to start this autumn term, George had squealed and danced around the kitchen, thrilled at the thought of her new adventure.

After she'd told her parents the news, she'd run all the way to the riding school to wrap her arms around

Timmy, giving him big hugs and kisses. After a lot of discussion, the riding school had agreed to loan him to George to take to Paddock Grove.

Over the summer, everything changed. The riding school was forced to shut down, and the horses sold off one by one. Everyone had been devastated by the news, but George had still held out a little hope…

As George fiddled with the end of Bear's lead rope, her mum told her how they'd talked to Mrs Hawksworth, the headmistress at Paddock Grove. She'd said that George could ride one of the school's own horses, but that the bond between horse and rider can make all the difference – especially for a rider with George's potential.

Her mum smiled encouragingly. "Mrs Hawksworth expects great things from you, George. She believes you can be a fantastic part of the school riding team. She said she hadn't seen such a natural rider in a long time, and now you've got Bear, imagine all the things you'll be able to achieve!"

George remained silent, a lump forming in her throat. How could Bear ever replace Timmy? It was going to be hard enough joining a new school in

Year Eight when everyone knew each other, let alone having to take Bear.

George's mum glanced at her watch. "Well, there's a lot still to do before tomorrow. We've got an early start if we need to be at Paddock Grove by two o'clock. It'll take a good eight or nine hours to get there if we have to stop a few times for Bear." She looked at Albert. "Before we get started, I've got a freshly baked Victoria sponge waiting in the kitchen if you fancy a piece with a cup of tea."

Albert grinned. "I'm never one to turn down a cuppa." He began to follow George's mum, who walked in the direction of their tiny stone cottage at the bottom of the lane.

"And *I* need to get the trunk down from the attic… Unless Bear fancies getting it down for me?" Her dad winked at George. "I'm sure by the time you've finished with Bear, he'll be show ready. You'll be able to ride him with pride."

George watched them go. She held her smile until they'd disappeared around the corner, then she let it drop and let out a long sigh. "Come on, Bear. Let's get you cleaned up." George tried to muster up some enthusiasm as she set to work preparing him for tomorrow.

Leading him to the fence, she tied him to the rusty ring on the post. Immediately, Bear began to fidget. He pulled at the rope, pawing at the ground while looking longingly at the grass beyond the gravel yard. "Stand still, Bear." She sighed impatiently. Then she went over to fill one of the old Stubbs buckets with water from the tap on the wall. She added a generous amount of shampoo, and the smell wafted up as she dipped the sponge from her grooming kit into the soapy water.

George wet Bear's thick coat then started scrubbing it with the soft, red rubber curry comb she had. The water and suds on Bear's back quickly turned black as the dirt and grime started to come away.

"Look how filthy you are," George tutted, and shook her head.

Bear flicked his tail impatiently, swishing shampoo everywhere as he fanned his body away from George.

"Stand still, Bear, it's only water," George muttered, and continued to work on the ingrained mud and grass stains on his coat. The white patches on him would take a lot more scrubbing and George decided that Bear was quite possibly the dirtiest pony she'd ever seen. Her arm quickly began to ache as she used large circular motions, working the comb through his coarse coat.

Once again, Bear shifted his weight, his eyes still fixed on the lush grass just beyond the yard while George carefully and gently worked through the tangles in his mane, wincing every time the comb snagged on a particularly stubborn knot.

As George moved to his tail, the warm breeze changed direction, carrying the scent of fresh grass to them, causing Bear's head to shoot up. His nostrils twitched as he smelt the aroma of it. Then he pulled at the rope harder, and with one big sudden yank, Bear tore the rusty ring from the rotting wooden post, setting himself free to barge past George. Head down, he cantered across the yard towards the field.

Caught off-guard, George stumbled backwards and crashed into the water bucket by her feet. She landed with a big splash, getting soaked from head to toe.

"Great." She wiped water from her face and shook her head. "Just great… *Thanks for that, Bear!*" Frustrated,

George shouted out the last words as Bear stood nearby, munching happily on the grass, looking very pleased with himself.

George sighed and watched him sadly. Bear's behaviour was the opposite of anything Timmy would do. Gosh, she missed everything about him – his kind eyes, his sleek coat, and how he seemed to understand her without her having to say a word. How would she ever love stubborn, wilful Bear the way she loved Timmy?

George felt a twinge in her chest, hoping his new owners, whoever they were, would love Timmy as much as she had. She hoped that he was happy, getting lots of scratches behind his ears, and that his night-time feed was a sloppy mix of chaff and hard food with a couple of apple slices and carrots in it. Just the way he liked it and just the way she'd always made it for him.

She squeezed her eyes closed, picturing herself on Timmy, then forced herself to snap them open. She got to her feet and trudged over to Bear with her clothes clinging uncomfortably to her skin.

"Can you *please*, please just behave yourself, Bear?" George stood in front of him with her hands on her hips, trying not to be too impatient with him. "We've got a big day tomorrow, and I'm already nervous enough, and this isn't helping at all." She gently took hold of Bear's head collar, led him back to the fence, and tied him to a post that looked more secure than the last. She'd have to tell Albert about the ring later.

"There. You're not going to escape from *that* knot." She shook her head and patted Bear on his back. Over the next hour George filled more buckets of water, washing more dirt away before using the sweat scraper from her grooming kit. She ran it over Bear's body, removing the excess water from his coat, then she used a soft cloth and dried his face, gently wiping around his eyes and ears.

Finally, she carefully held each foot and, using the brand-new hoof pick, she cleaned out Bear's hooves. She removed any stones and mud lodged between his frogs and around the edges of his shoes, while Bear continued to fidget, trying to snatch his foot away.

"Oh no you don't, Bear!" Panting, she held on tightly. Bear wasn't the only one who could be stubborn. "You are having your feet cleaned whether you like it or not. It's not good for you to leave all those stones in there."

George continued to hang on, making sure Bear's hooves were cleaned out and spotless, and at last, tired but pleased, she stepped back to look at the results of her hard work. She smiled at him.

"Who knew you could look this clean, hey?" She gave him a scratch on his withers. Bear's black-and-white coat shone in the late afternoon sun. He looked almost presentable. "Dad should've taken a photo of you looking like this," she laughed.

In return, Bear shook himself, droplets of water flying everywhere.

As the sun set, George led Bear back to the stable, checking he had enough water and haylage for the night. Then, with a mix of emotions and a very big yawn, she slowly walked back towards the cottage.

Despite everything that had happened, despite her disappointment over Bear, she felt a tingle of excitement as she thought about tomorrow. Her dreams were really coming true… Oh my gosh. She – Georgia Harris! – was *actually* going to be a pupil at Paddock Grove!

Suddenly she let out a delighted giggle and whirled around and around and around on the spot, looking up at the sky. A new school, a new start, a new adventure lay ahead…

Chapter Three

TRUNKS, TACK AND TAKE-OFF

"*Georgia! Georgia! George*, are you up yet, sweetheart? We don't want to be late."

It was the next morning and George's mum was calling for her up the stairs.

"I won't be long, I promise!" George answered as she stood in her small bedroom. The early morning sunshine was just starting to peek through the curtains, casting a rich pinkish light across posters of George's favourite famous show jumpers on the walls, rosettes from her competitions that hung from the wooden beams, and her bookshelf crammed with horse books. It would be weeks before she saw them all again, and excitement and nerves bubbled inside her.

She hadn't been able to sleep much last night and had got up early to wash her long brown curly hair, which was now tied back in a loose ponytail. The school had several different uniforms for all the different activities, and since she was taking Bear to the school with her, George had dressed in her new Paddock Grove riding uniform – jodhpurs, polo shirt, and the school jumper with its badge sewn on the front, which bore the school's motto: "Together in Triumph".

There came a soft tap on the door, then her mum's head peeked around. "All set for the big day?"

George nodded. "I think so." As butterflies fluttered in her stomach, she added, "I hope so. I'm a bit worried that everyone in my year will know each other."

George's mum stepped into the room and took George's hands in hers. "I know it's hard starting a new school, and even harder to do that in Year Eight, but you always make friends everywhere you go – at school, at the pony club. You even made friends when we went on our camping holiday last year, didn't you?" She smiled. "I promise, you'll soon settle in."

George took a deep breath. She was going to miss

all her friends from her old school but going to Paddock Grove was a once-in-a-lifetime chance. "You really think it'll be alright?"

Her mum laughed warmly. "I *know* it'll be alright." She gave George a hug. "So, Dad's already loaded the bags and trunk onto the lorry. All we need now are you and Bear." She paused, and George saw a glint of tears. "We'll miss you terribly, and the cottage won't be the same without you, but we're so proud of you, George."

She gently let go of George's hands to dab her eyes with a tissue. "Now, how about some breakfast? I've made some scrambled eggs and toast. That's if Albert's left any." She laughed again.

George couldn't even think of eating. Her stomach was doing knots. "I'll be down in a minute if that's OK. I'm just saying my goodbyes to my room."

Her mum nodded. "I'll leave you to it."

Once her mum disappeared, George had one last glance around, then she pulled on her well-worn riding boots, grabbed her new school rucksack and took another deep breath. Then, touching the badge on her jumper, she made her way downstairs.

Half an hour later, and feeling much calmer, George made her way quickly to the sheep shed. The early morning sky was turning from pale pink to pale blue, and a gentle breeze rustled the leaves in the trees as she made her way along the pretty country lane. The village of Hedgedale in the North Yorkshire Moors – and their little stone cottage with its white picket fence – was the only home she'd ever known. She loved this place, but though she would miss it fiercely, she couldn't wait to explore the tracks and bridleways around Paddock Grove, which was nestled near the Jurassic Coast in Dorset, surrounded by amazing white sandy beaches and rolling countryside. It was the perfect place for riding. The perfect place for going to school.

George continued to walk, her shoes crunching on the gravel path which led to Albert's farm, but as she neared the shed, George froze. Oh no! The rickety old door of the shed hung open, broken.

Bear was gone.

Gone!

George whirled round as panic began to rise in her

chest. "Bear? *Bear?*" She ran to the lane to see if he was there, but not being able to spot him, she dashed back to the yard, looking around. "Bear, Bear, where are you?" Oh no, this couldn't be happening. Where was he?

Then she heard a noise to her left. She darted towards the sound and sprinted around the large tractor shed, passing the old tabby cat basking in the early morning sun. And there was Bear, happily eating one of the hay bales piled up nearby.

"Oh Bear, thank goodness." But then she stared at him harder, open-mouthed. "Bear, *no*! Oh no! *Bear!*" Mud covered his white patches that she'd worked so hard to scrub clean yesterday. He'd clearly rolled, and sticky burrs and haylage were tangled in his mane and tail.

"Oh my goodness."

George jumped at her mum's voice as she walked up behind her.

She whirled round. "Mum, what am I going to do now? I *can't* take him looking like that."

Her mum seemed very relaxed about Bear's appearance. She smiled. "He'll clean up fine, sweetheart."

"But look at him!" This time, George couldn't hide

her disappointment. She'd wanted him to look perfect. She'd wanted everything about today to be perfect, and now Bear had spoilt it.

"George, don't look so worried, it's only some mud."

"But he's a mess. He's … he's…" George was so upset she couldn't find her words. The excitement of the journey ahead, of the day ahead, of everything she'd worked so hard for, started to fade away. Wiping away any tears, George muttered, "I'll clean him now. Hopefully it won't take too long."

Her mum glanced at her watch. "I'm afraid we haven't got time, George. We need to be there by three. We're cutting it fine already. He'll have to go like that."

"Like that?" George couldn't believe what she was hearing. "No, no, he can't… He can't go like that. There's no way." She shook her head furiously and had a sudden thought: it would be better if they left him here altogether! But as soon as the idea popped into her mind, George pushed it aside. She was being ungrateful, she knew that. Her parents would be so upset if they thought she didn't want Bear.

She glanced over at him. Maybe she could give him

a quick once-over with the dandy brush to take the worst off.

Her dad rounded the corner then, grinning as he pushed back his dreadlocks. "George, your transport awaits! It's all ready. Albert loaded it up with haylage and water this morning, so we can just go, go, go." He laughed and nodded towards the gates.

Just when George thought things couldn't get worse, an old, dirty sheep lorry, held together in places with silver gaffer tape, chugged around the corner. George stared in horror. *This* was to be their transport? What had happened to the riding school's horsebox they were going to use?

As if reading her mind, George's dad smiled. "Unfortunately, there's a buyer coming to look at the riding school's horsebox today. Albert was kind enough to let us use his sheep lorry." Her dad waved to Albert, who sat behind the wheel, puffing on his pipe. "So come on, George, load him up." He rubbed his hands excitedly. "This is going to be some adventure."

George turned away and rolled her eyes. That was certainly one way of putting it…

Chapter Four

NEW BEGINNINGS

The drive from Hedgedale to Paddock Grove was much longer and more tiring than George thought it was going to be. Not only did the lorry smell of pipe smoke and wet sheep, they'd also stopped several times on the way, checking Bear, who seemed quite content with his large bag of haylage and garlic Likit. (They also made some bathroom stops for Albert, who'd drunk several flasks of tea that George's mum had made for the journey.)

George was quiet most of the way, but her parents and Albert made up for it by singing at the top of their voices, every single song they could possibly remember. Songs George had never heard of and, from the way the adults sang them, never wanted to hear again.

After leaving the motorway, they drove hour after hour down winding country lanes, with the warm breeze whispering through the early autumn fields and flowers. Then they turned for the coast, driving along roads framed by jutting cliffs and windswept stretches of golden beach, while the September sun bounced off the water, turning the ocean into a glistening flat jewel.

George couldn't quite believe it was happening. Everything seemed like the perfect dream. She'd always loved horses. Always. She couldn't actually remember a time when she wasn't thinking about them, dreaming about them or even drawing them. Since she was old enough, she'd spent all her free time at the riding stables, just enjoying being around the horses as well as mucking out and doing the chores no one else wanted to do – work she'd have done with or without free lessons in return. Now she'd won a place at Paddock Grove, her world would be on repeat: live, breathe and dream horses.

George sighed contentedly as they finally turned towards the little village of Willowbrook, which was only a couple of miles from the school.

As they rounded the next bend, George caught her breath. The view was even more amazing than she remembered from when she came months ago for her interview. Ahead were rolling green hills dotted with grazing horses, and George imagined herself galloping across the fields criss-crossed by bridle paths.

In the distance, George spotted a glint of blue – the sea! She'd forgotten how close the school was to the coast, which meant she'd be able to ride through the sea. She'd always wanted to, and she imagined herself galloping along the surf's edge, the sun above and the wind in her face. She knew it would feel something like magic.

They passed a couple of tiny villages and several large equine properties, and George spun round excitedly when she spotted a large sign for Clear Fields, the boys' equestrian boarding school. This was truly horse country!

"It says in the welcome pack that this lane can get cut off when the weather's bad," her mum shouted over the sound of the engine. "The river floods over, blocking the road."

"It's beautiful," George whispered breathlessly as they splashed through the ford.

At the top of the biggest hill, George's heart jumped as she looked down and saw Paddock Grove. The school grounds stretched further than she could see, and as they neared the tall, imposing wrought-iron gates, George tried to stop herself feeling queasy.

Maybe she was being silly, but now it had come to it, she wasn't quite as confident as she'd been before they'd set off. It was real now: this was going to be her home during term time for the next four years.

"Are you alright, George?" Her mum swivelled round to smile at her. For a moment Mum didn't say anything, then she lowered her voice into a warm whisper. "I promise you'll be fine."

"She'll be more than fine," her dad – who'd been sneezing a lot of the journey from his allergy – added. "She'll be great. Our George earned her place." He looked across the back seat and gave George a wink. "You've worked hard to be here."

George smiled gratefully, though that didn't stop her feeling shaky as they drove through the gates. A wide gravel driveway swept up to the school, lined with perfectly trimmed hedges and colourful flower beds.

The place was *spectacular.*

The main building was a huge converted stately home, majestic against the landscape. The spotless limestone walls of Paddock Grove stretched upwards, topped by tall, elegant chimneys and a beautiful clock tower that caught the afternoon rays of sunlight. Even from where she sat in the lorry, George could see the grand entrance's enormous doors, which had large brass carvings of horses standing either side.

Her gaze darted around. Other buildings spread out across the grounds – accommodation for the staff and students, along with the modern teaching blocks and stables – but it was really the high-tech equestrian facilities that made George's heart soar.

In the gaps between the buildings she could just about spot the outdoor arena, its sandy surface raked smooth and perfect for jumping. Beyond it lay the fields and paddocks, separated by sturdy wooden post-and-rail fences. To the east were the visitors' stables, then the path to the main yard, and although she couldn't see them, the indoor school and not one but *two* more arenas. Beyond that was the cross-country course, the woods and the bridle paths. George couldn't wait to explore it all…

The lorry came to a grinding, noisy halt in the parking area, sending plumes of smoke from its exhaust into the air. It looked entirely out of place beside the gleaming silver horsebox they'd parked next to. George tried not to be embarrassed (but she was).

She glanced out of the window, breathing in the air, which held the unmistakable smell of horses, but she quickly turned away as she spotted a group of girls staring and giggling. They were all dressed in the same smart jodhpurs and pale-blue polo shirts as George wore. (Although their uniforms looked immaculate, making her overly aware of her own travel-crumpled appearance.)

She wiped the crumbs off her jodhpurs from the biscuit she'd eaten when they'd stopped earlier. "Mum?"

Her mum turned around again.

"Are you sure it'll be alright?" She was so nervous.

Her mum nodded and reached over, pushing a strand of George's corkscrew hair out of her eyes. "It's like Dad says: you'll be great. Everyone gets nervous as well as excited when they're starting a new school. Just remember, everything you need is within you, poppet."

George smiled. She was never quite sure what her mum *actually meant* when she said that, but it always made George feel better.

"Right then, you untie Bear, and I'll open the ramp," Albert suggested loudly.

Shuffling through the cabin into the back where Bear was, George untied his rope from the ring. He took no notice of her and continued to eat his haylage, though as it happened, George paid little attention to him either, lost in a daydream of what it would have been like to bring Timmy here and wondering what he was doing now.

The ramp of the lorry clanged down, breaking off George's thoughts. Albert leant on the side and nodded towards Bear. "You're lucky he's not fussed by anything; a lot of horses are spooked by their own shadow." Albert stared at her from under his bushy eyebrows. He frowned, and George thought she heard a slight tone of concern in his voice. "Mind, if you want to build a bond with him, you've got to do more than just feed and water him. He'll never be the pony you want him to be if you ignore him."

George felt her cheeks heating up. She didn't want to be rude and say, *He isn't the pony I want now or ever*, so she just smiled, hoping that Albert wouldn't say any more. She was both surprised and ashamed that Albert had noticed the way she'd been behaving towards Bear.

Turning away from the old farmer, George gave a gentle tug on the lead rope. Bear didn't move. She tried again, but the most Bear did was shift his weight from one hind leg to the other and stare at George, unimpressed.

"Bear, come on. *Bear*, we've got to go..." She could hear the plaintive whine in her voice. *"Bear."*

"It's no good getting irritated with him, lass. He'll only pick up on your mood and wonder what he's done wrong. It won't get him to move any faster," Albert said. (Very unhelpfully, George thought.)

"I know what I'm doing, Albert," George replied,

wishing that Albert would go away and pulling a little harder on Bear's lead rope at the same time. She'd unboxed Timmy plenty of times when they went to competitions, so she knew what she was doing. It was Bear who was the problem.

"Please, Bear, not now," she whispered desperately. Then, not unkindly, she pulled and coaxed him some more, and even tried bribing him with a nut treat she had in her pocket, but Bear remained like a statue.

"Is that really her horse?" A tall girl with blonde hair, standing by the lorry, snorted with laughter. "I've seen ponies at fairs that look better than that!"

George's cheeks burnt again as she glanced at the other students, their beautiful horses looking glossy in the sunlight as they calmly walked them towards the stable blocks. Just when George thought Bear might refuse to move altogether, he caught sight of something. His ears pricked up, he spun around, and with a sudden flash of excitement, Bear bolted forward.

George yelped.

Stumbling, she tried to keep her balance, but it was no use. Bear was too strong. He trotted at speed down the ramp, dragging George with him off the ramp and onto the tarmac, as laughter erupted from the gathered students.

"Bear, *stop*! Bear!"

But now Bear had got started, he had no intention of stopping. He hauled George across the parking area, heading towards the grassy flower bed. He had a broad chest and a strong neck, so no amount of weight on the rope would stop him as he barged past a family saying goodbye to each other beside a very expensive car, causing them to jump out of the way while George continued to hang on.

"Bear, *stop*! Bear, steady! Bear! *No!*" George shouted as she tried desperately to ignore the look of horror on everyone's faces as they flashed past her.

She nosedived into the gravel, tumbling over to land head first in a bush by the wall, where she lay very still with her eyes closed. She wasn't going to ever open them. Humiliation rushed through her. Even from where she was lying, she could hear a loud buzz of laughter.

"Did you see that? She got dragged off by her own horse!"

"What a mess!"

The laughter continued to rise. But George found none of it funny. None of it *at all.* This wasn't how her first day was supposed to go. This would never have happened with Timmy.

Still lying on the ground, George heard a sudden, sharp clap echo across the courtyard, silencing the laughter. She opened her eyes and sat up to look at the formidable figure striding towards her. George wasn't the only one: Mrs Hawksworth, the headmistress of Paddock Grove, commanded the attention of *everyone* present. Even the parents.

In her fifties, Mrs Hawksworth wore a no-nonsense, tweed two-piece suit with a green gilet over it, and a matching fedora hat with a peacock feather brooch attached. She looked like she'd stepped out of the pages of *Horse & Hound.*

"Girls, girls! That is quite enough!" Mrs Hawksworth had a presence which demanded respect. Her aristocratic accent cut through the air, silencing students and adults alike. "This is not how we behave at Paddock Grove."

The girls who'd been laughing all became serious under Mrs Hawksworth's steely gaze. She turned her attention to George, who was struggling to untangle herself from the bush.

“Miss Harris.” Mrs Hawksworth’s tone was brisk but not unkind. “You and your pony have made *quite* the entrance.”

George wanted the ground to swallow her up. “I’m sorry … Bear just—”

“No need for apologies.” Mrs Hawksworth held up a hand for silence. “But you will have to work on your discipline. We do not tolerate ill-mannered ponies here at Paddock Grove.”

Deflated, George nodded. “Yes, Mrs Hawksworth.”

Mrs Hawksworth’s expression softened slightly as George finally untangled herself from the bush and got to her feet. She brushed the leaves off herself.

“Good. Now, let’s get this situation under control and make sure – Bear, isn’t it? – is settled properly.” Mrs Hawksworth’s voice was firm but friendly. “Miss Travis...? Yes, you, Jessica.” She signalled to a girl who George thought looked very sophisticated and slightly older than her. She was tall and slim, and her brown, shiny hair was cut into a short bob. “I’d be grateful if you could assist our newcomer and help settle Bear into his stable. He'll be in the Ascot barn."

"Yes, Mrs Hawksworth."

As Mrs Hawksworth looked over to watch another horse being unloaded, George noticed Jessica roll her eyes and smirk at the group of friends she was standing with before she walked over, looking very unenthusiastic.

Mrs Hawksworth turned back to George. "Miss Harris, you may find that a patient manner makes a willing horse." She glanced around at the other pupils, who remained silent. "Remember, girls, strive for excellence, in and out of the saddle." And with those words, Mrs Hawksworth strode off.

George and her parents gathered by the lorry for farewells while Albert held Bear so George could say goodbye. The school staff had taken her things inside, and with Jessica standing a short distance away tapping her foot impatiently, George didn't feel like she could take very long.

"Just be yourself and do your best," George's mum said as her tears flowed. "Home is just a phone call away –

but remember that you're here to follow your dreams… And as for you and Bear, you two will soon figure it out."

George was afraid to speak in case she cried as well, and she gave her dad a hug, who gave her the biggest one back.

Albert handed George Bear's lead rope and tipped his hat, looking very watery-eyed himself as George's mum got into the lorry, glancing back over her shoulder towards Jessica. "You will take care of my daughter, won't you?"

Jessica gave a tight smile, but she didn't say anything as George watched the lorry sputter to life. Before George had a chance to wave one last goodbye, Jessica marched up to her.

"Well? Are you going to stand there like your lump of a pony, or do you want to go to the stables?"

Chapter Five

SETTLING IN

“That’s Mr Thatcher, the yard manager,” Jessica said, pointing to a tall, stern-looking man. She marched moodily ahead of George. “He’ll tell you where to put your donkey.”

“But—”

Jessica spun and looked at George coldly as she stood holding Bear in the middle of the horse yard. “But what?” she snapped.

“I–I thought you...” Feeling awful from the disastrous start to what was supposed to be a perfect new adventure, George trailed off.

“*You thought* I was going to babysit you?” Jessica laughed, meanly. “Well, you thought wrong. I’ve got better things to do than look after kids and...” She screwed up her face over dramatically. "That thing."

Jessica stormed off, leaving George and Bear by the rows of stable blocks. What was she supposed to do now? She certainly didn't want to have to go and find Mrs Hawksworth. That would be awful. Sighing, she glanced around to speak to Mr Thatcher, but he'd disappeared too. George was beginning to think the whole idea of coming to Paddock Grove was a mistake. She didn't belong here, and she doubted she'd ever fit in.

Bear nudged her as she looked to see if anyone else was around, but the yard was completely empty. She sighed. Trying not to get upset, George was stroking Bear's velvet nose when she suddenly remembered that Mrs Hawksworth had said Bear was in the barn.

Spotting it, she led Bear slowly towards it. Inside, each stable had a laminated nameplate in a frame on the door, and George walked down the row of horses to the one before last. In large, black italic lettering, there was his name:

BEAR

George turned to him. "Here we are, Bear. This is your

new home. What do you think?" She led him inside and, even though George was feeling low, she smiled at how beautiful it was. It was huge and modern, with a window at the back for Bear to look out, and between his stall and the ones on either side were metal bars that allowed the horses to see each other. There was an automatic water filler in the corner and Bear's bed was made up of thick, fluffy white woodchips that smelt of lavender.

Once George had taken his head collar off, Bear immediately made his way to the large bag of haylage hanging up. He looked very content. George, however, felt the opposite. This would be the first time she'd ever been away from her parents, besides the time when she'd been at pony camp, and she wasn't sure how she'd feel tonight. All the other girls in her dormitory would be used to being away from home – they'd already had a whole year to get used to it.

George suddenly burst into tears. She walked over to Bear and hugged him, smelling the faint hint of shampoo on him as she buried her head into his neck. He let out a small whinny, which made George cry harder.

"Hi."

George jumped at the voice behind her. Upset, she turned around and quickly wiped away her tears.

A girl who looked the same age as George smiled. Her freckled face held nothing but warmth. "I'm Katie. I saw Jessica walking out of the yard, so I wanted to come and see how you were doing."

George smiled back shyly. "Thanks… I don't think she was very happy that Mrs Hawksworth asked her to help me."

"Jess never wants to help anyone." Katie rolled her eyes.

"Oh, I'm Georgia by the way, but everyone just calls me George, and this…" She sighed. "This is Bear." She nodded towards him.

Katie giggled. "Hello, Bear. You're quite the character, aren't you?" She glanced back at George. "The first week is always the hardest, but you'll soon forget all about home."

George couldn't imagine that would ever be true.

"Everyone's heard about you," Katie said suddenly.

"Me?"

Katie nodded and spoke kindly. "There's always

hundreds of girls trying to get in for every year group, and everyone's talking about how *you* must be the most brilliant rider."

George flushed.

"Did you take the test on Bear?"

"No! *No!* He's..." Embarrassed, she shrugged. "I only got Bear because Mum and Dad couldn't afford to buy the horse I wanted. Bear, well, he's..."

Katie looked at her the way Albert had done, and George felt slightly ashamed at the way she was behaving towards Bear.

"He's different to Timmy, the horse I used to loan – he was my best friend," George finally said.

Katie glanced at Bear. "You'll get used to him; he seems really sweet."

George didn't say anything, although she didn't know how Katie could think that Bear was sweet after he'd dragged her off the lorry in front of everyone. Even now she could feel the embarrassment.

"I've never had to change horses," Katie added thoughtfully. "Sheriff's the only horse I've ever owned. I can't imagine how it would be to see him sold on. You and Bear will be a great team. Things just take time. Come on." Katie smiled warmly again. "Why don't I show you around the yard and you can see where everything is?"

"I'd like that… thank you," George said.

Stepping out into the yard, George started to feel much better, and this time when she looked around she was able to really appreciate how beautiful it all was. The Monarch stables at Paddock Grove were modern and the nicest she'd ever seen. The stables at her riding school were old brick and wood, but these were new with enormous blocks of loose boxes around the sides in addition to the central barn where Bear was stabled.

All of the stables had beautiful sliding wooden doors a rich chestnut colour that gleamed in the sun. Every one of them was equipped with automatic water systems and mounted feeders, and lined with rubber matting covered in fluffy, clean woodchips.

On the day of the interview, the stables had been a blur of excitement and nerves. Now, walking around with Katie and taking it all in properly, George realized just how lucky she was, and her stomach fluttered again with a familiar sense of excitement.

She sighed contentedly, glancing at the weathered stone mounting block in the centre of the yard, its surface smooth and worn in contrast to the modern stables around it.

Katie saw George looking and said, "That's been there since the main house was built a couple of hundred years ago or so. When they changed this place into a school in the 1940s, they decided to leave it there."

They strolled through the stable yard, their feet clicking on smooth cobblestones.

"How many horses are there?" George asked as they walked past curious horses looking out over their doors.

"About a hundred," Katie said. "There's seventy horses owned by the students and thirty by the school. The school's horses are for anyone who couldn't bring one of their own."

"It's a shame not everyone can bring their horse."

Katie nodded. "Not everyone has their own horse – and there isn't enough space for everyone who does. Stable space only opens up when someone who had a riding place leaves, so getting to bring your horse is pretty competitive. You have get a minimum score in the entrance exam *and* be amazing in the ridden test. There's always people who miss out – places to bring your horse are like gold dust, but thankfully once you've got your horse here, it stays as long as you keep up with classes and caring for them." Katie gave George a curious look. "Newbies only get a chance if there's still space after the riders who are already here have been offered it, or if you're an *exceptional* rider and impress Mrs Hawksworth and the head riding coach." She glanced at George and gently bumped her as they walked. "Which *you* clearly did."

George could feel herself blush again. She knew Katie was being kind, but it made her feel anxious. Worried. The riding test she'd done was on Timmy, so how could she impress anyone on Bear? Especially since she'd never actually ridden him!

Katie pointed out the hay barn and the feed room, as well as the place to wash down the horses, before she pointed to a smaller stone building that stood further back from the rest.

"That's what we call Mr Mannington's shop … although he doesn't let anyone in it. The only time you'll ever see him get cross is if he finds any girls in there. He's the farrier and he comes down once a week. You'll like him," she said, her eyes twinkling. "Everyone does."

George peeked inside the farrier's workshop. Metal tools hung neatly on the wall – hammers, tongs, and various hoof rasps for filing hooves. In the corner stood the unlit forge, the oven, where she guessed the farrier heated the metal and made and shaped horseshoes.

Once they'd done a circuit of the indoor and outdoor schools, George marvelling at the stacks of colourful poles and wings tucked neatly away ready for jumping lessons, and Katie had pointed out where the cross-country course was along with the fields and bridleways, they looped back round to where Bear was stabled.

"So what do the other girls do when there's riding lessons? The ones who haven't got horses?" George asked as they walked back to Bear and Katie's horse Sheriff, who was stabled in the same block.

"The timetable's planned so that anyone not in a riding lesson has stable management and equine health classes – whether you have a horse or not, you still have the same number of lessons. But they have to book to ride the school's horses outside of their scheduled lessons."

As they neared Bear, George saw a tall girl with long, straight, glossy black hair pulled into a high ponytail. She was standing outside the stable where Bear was poking his head out, her brown eyes narrowing.

"That's Meg." Katie pulled a face and whispered, "She's in the year above… She's such a pain. She's friends with Jess and they all think they rule the school – even though they're only a year older, they think they can boss us about."

"What on earth is this?" Meg demanded, her American accent sharp in the quiet yard. She gave Bear a look of total disgust before she turned to scowl at Katie and George. "Why is he here?"

The way Meg stood with her smart clothes and snooty expression gave her an air of sophistication that made George shrink back slightly, but Katie stepped forward with a sigh. "That's Bear, George's pony." She gestured towards George. "She's new."

"Well, that thing can't stay here; I don't want him

next to my horse," Meg snapped. "Oh my gosh, look, it's trying to touch Ophelia! Shoo, go away!" She waved her arms dramatically at Bear who (as George would expect) took no notice.

Sure enough, Bear stretched his muzzle through the bars that divided each stable, curiously sniffing the tall, gleaming bay mare in the stable next to his.

"He's just being friendly," Katie said firmly.

Meg clearly wasn't impressed. "Friendly? I don't want a thing like that to be friendly."

Katie shrugged. "Ophelia doesn't seem to mind."

"Well, *I* mind…"

"Well, you would, wouldn't you?" Katie muttered, which made George smile.

"Did you say something?" Meg stared hard at Katie, then sniffed haughtily. "He's sure to give Ophelia fleas or feather mites or something! Yuk." Meg's voice rose louder as she crossed her arms and pouted. "And who buys a piebald pony anyway?" she sneered. "Do you know how much my horse cost? More than you could even imagine. This is so not OK. I'm going to speak to Mr Thatcher and Mrs Hawksworth right now."

Meg marched off, striding across the yard in her expensive-looking blue patent riding boots.

Katie turned to George with a reassuring smile. "Ignore her. She's always like that. She goes through horses like shoes."

George didn't understand. "What do you mean?"

"Well, she gets these beautiful horses, and if they don't do what she wants, instead of practising with them, she just gets a different horse."

George was shocked. "Doesn't she care about them at all?"

Katie pulled a face. "Well, she's not mean to them ever, but I think with Meg it's all about the way she looks. They're like a fashion accessory. She's a great rider, but like I say, she and her friends think they own the school. Don't listen to anything they have to say. Bear's got just as much right to be here as any horse."

George wasn't entirely sure about that … but then, without Timmy she wasn't sure that *she* deserved to be here either. Still, she'd hated hearing Meg say such mean things about Bear when he hadn't done anything wrong other than exist.

She wandered over to Bear and stroked his neck as he stuck his head out to greet her, then she looked at Ophelia. She was a beautiful dark bay, at least 17 hands in height. Powerful and athletic-looking. Her coat had a glossy finish, and her short black mane and long tail were thick and silky.

George turned back to scruffy old Bear. "Hey Bear, you seem like you've made a friend already." She spoke warmly to him and smiled as he nuzzled her hand. "I hope you're going to like it here."

George waited to feel an inkling of that bond she'd felt with Timmy, but she didn't feel anything apart from sadness and guilt. She felt really bad that she didn't want him, not just because her parents would be upset, but because it wasn't fair for Bear. He deserved an owner who loved him the way she'd loved Timmy.

"Do you want to stay here longer? I think I've shown you everything! Or we can go to the school? I can introduce you to some of the other girls, who are *nothing* like Meg."

"Bear's not on the school's livery programme," George said. "I'm on a full scholarship, so I'll have to do all the mucking out and feeding. Maybe I should bed him down now and join you later?"

She looked at the fluffy, white woodchip bed Bear was standing on. It shouldn't take her long. She was used to mucking out several stables at the riding school and, compared to that, one stall with a fresh bed shouldn't be too difficult.

"On the first day and first morning, the yard staff tend to all the horses," Katie said with a grin. "Which feels like a holiday for me. Even when I'm home for the actual holidays, I've got to muck out and skip out, turn out, catch in, make sure there's no ragwort in the fields, poo pick, *everything*." She laughed then. "Mum says there's no days off when it comes to horses, so I've been caring for Sheriff long before I came to Paddock Grove. Though I wouldn't have it any other way. He was homebred by my gran, so I've known him since he was a foal…" Katie nodded to the stable on the other side of Bear. "That's Sheriff."

George leant forward, surprised she hadn't noticed the light bay gelding who was standing quietly at the back of his stable on the other side of Bear's. Like all the horses George had seen since arriving at Paddock Grove, Sheriff was taller than Bear – not by much, but he was definitely slimmer and more athletic.

"He's such a good boy." Katie beamed proudly, blowing him a kiss.

As George watched, Sheriff turned towards them. His eyes were warm and dark, and he had a white stripe that stood out against the light bay of his coat.

"Wow," George whispered. "He's gorgeous."

"Thanks. He can be a bit shy with new people, but he's so gentle, and I'm sure he and Bear will get on brilliantly." She gave George a shy glance as she added, "A bit like us… Come on, let's go to the dorm and I'll show you some of the school along the way, though I know it's a lot to take in."

George scratched Bear's face. His eyes were big pools of curiosity. "Goodnight, Bear." She sighed. "It's been a long day for you too, hasn't it? It's all as new for you as it is for me – only I know what's happening, and you don't." Once again, she surprised herself with the sudden warmth she felt towards him.

Chapter Six

A WHISTLE-STOP TOUR

"Oh, did they send you the term timetable?" Katie wondered cheerfully. "If you haven't got it, we can print you a copy in the school library. You'll love the library – it's huge – they've got every single horse book and manual you could imagine."

"I wasn't sent it," George mumbled and tried to stop herself feeling overwhelmed as she watched all the girls chatting and milling about.

"OK then, let's go round this way."

Thankful for the distraction from her worries about Bear and missing her parents, George hurried to keep up with Katie. As they walked, Katie continued to talk.

"...and this is the front hall and stairs, although you're not allowed to use them unless the school's putting on a special occasion. Only the teachers and sixth formers can use them; everyone else has to use the back stairs, which are over there."

Katie pointed as George tried to take it all in. The grand entrance hall was nothing like her scruffy village school. Here, high ceilings loomed above her, and the wide oak staircase with a thick red tartan carpet swept upwards. Polished wooden floors gleamed underfoot, and the walls were decorated with huge paintings of horses in gilded gold frames.

"That way's the dining hall," Katie continued to chatter, "and down that hallway are some of the classrooms. There's teaching blocks over the courtyard – you can see the orchard and the arenas from the science labs. And further up is where the cross-country course is, and all the bridle paths. The accommodation block is in a whole separate building. You'll see that later." She turned. "Then down that corridor is the school office and the bursar's office, but make sure you don't run or shout when you go past his door, otherwise he'll give you detention." She rolled her eyes. "Mr Bassey is *very* strict."

George nodded. How would she ever remember

where everything was and who everyone was?

Katie seemed to pick up on George's nerves. "Don't worry, you'll get the hang of it all. Right now, just remember that girls are divided up into different houses – you're in the same house and dorm as me."

George was delighted by this news. It felt like a great relief.

"The houses are called after famous horses. Seabiscuit, Frankel, Milton, Stroller. We're in Stroller – which is the perfect house for you!"

George looked puzzled.

"Stroller's named after the only pony to have competed at the Olympics. He was only 14.1 hands – about the same as Bear – and won silver at the 1968 Olympics in Mexico. So you and Bear have a lot to live up to," she laughed.

"I'm so used to my small secondary school; everything here seems so big."

Katie gave her a sympathetic smile. "I know the grounds are huge but there are only about three hundred students here. Each year has two forms with thirty-ish people in each, but a lot of the field management and riding lessons are combined, so you'll find yourself mixing with most of the others at some point or other. It's nice!"

"So, do you share a dorm with everyone in your form?"

"No – dorms are sorted by house."

This was all so confusing. George's head was beginning to hurt with all the new information.

Katie looked at George and burst into laughter. "Information overload! Sorry! You don't have to remember any of this. If you get stuck, just ask me. But the forms are for school and classes; your house is the building where you live, and the people who live there are a bit like your family, going from Year Seven right up to Year Eleven. There's seventy-five people in each house, and each dorm room sleeps four or five. You'll be sharing with me and two other girls."

George grinned. That was the best news. She was so pleased that she'd be sharing a room with Katie – she liked her a lot already.

"There's a lot of rivalry between each house," Katie continued. "At the end of each term, the house with the most riding points wins a prize, but the main aim is to have the most points come the end of the year, which is announced at prize-giving on the last day of the summer term. Whichever one wins gets a cup with the house name engraved on it. Frankel has won six times in the past ten years." Katie rolled her eyes, then grinned. "Maybe you and Bear are going to bring Stroller House luck."

"I'm not sure about that," Looking to change the subject away from Bear, George thought back to what Katie had said about how competitive it was to be allowed to bring your own horse. "You must be a great rider if you're here on a riding place."

"Yeah, but I was lucky to get in. I think it helped that my gran was one of the travelling vets for the major tournaments Mrs Hawksworth used to compete in."

George hurried to keep up with Katie, who strode towards the library through another long hallway lined with large windows and looking out across fields.

"Mrs Hawksworth can ride?" George was surprised. She hadn't mentioned anything about it at the interview even though they'd talked a lot about horses.

"She still rides now. She's amazing, and you should see her horse, Storm. He's a beautiful black 17-hand Thoroughbred stallion. He's fiery though, and I don't think he'd let anyone else ride him apart from Mrs Hawksworth. He won't let most people go near him. He's kept separately from most of the other horses," Katie laughed, and George couldn't help liking her more and more.

They hurried past all the girls' trunks taking up space in the gym, and George noticed a glass cabinet full of trophies and rosettes the school riding team had won. It was George's dream to ride for Paddock Grove against other schools, but already her dream was beginning to fade because of Bear. She was sure that she and Bear weren't going to do anything more than put up with each other.

Katie might believe they would bring Stroller House luck, but George suspected that if Stroller's name made it onto the house cup, it wouldn't be because of her or Bear.

Chapter Seven

ROOM-MATES AND RIDING BOOTS

"This is us," Katie said, pushing open one of the doors at the end of the corridor. "Welcome to your new home!"

George stepped inside and inwardly gasped. The room was huge, with big windows that looked out over the stables and fields. Four beds stood against the walls, each with its own little nightstand and a shelf above. There were rosettes and photos of horses next to each bed, apart from the one at the end by the window.

"That one's yours." Katie pointed to the empty bed. "You can put your things up on the shelf and pinboard. Your trunk's in the dressing room through there" – George glanced towards a doorway in the corner – "where the drawers and wardrobe are."

Feeling nervous, George's mind wandered to her mum and dad. She wasn't exactly homesick, but she could certainly do with the comfort of having her parents there right now.

There were two other girls in the room – one with short red hair who was carefully arranging her riding trophies, and another with a long dark braid, sprawled on her bed, reading a book.

"Hey guys, this is George," Katie announced. "George, meet Tabitha." The red-headed girl looked up from her trophies, her green eyes intense. "And that's Lilieta, but she prefers to be called Lili."

"Nice to meet you," Tabitha said quietly, her tone not exactly cool, but not particularly warm. George had the sense she was someone who was hard to impress.

Lili, on the other hand, bounced up from her bed with a big smile. "Hello! I'm so pleased you're here. We all voted you should have the bed by the window – it's the best view."

Tabitha sighed. "Not *all* of us voted that."

"Stop being so grumpy." Lili's nose crinkled up as

she laughed loudly. "You're just cross that everyone's talking about how brilliant a rider George is."

George really wished everyone would stop talking about her being so good – especially if it was making people jealous. She almost felt like blurting out the truth that she was only good because of Timmy, but Tabitha had already turned her back to finish sorting out her shelf.

"And that doesn't worry you?" Tabitha tutted.

"No. Why should it?" George was struck by Lili's warm smile and friendly brown eyes that seemed to sparkle with mischief. She was taller than George, with a deep, sandy complexion.

"Because part of the reason we're here is to compete against each other," Tabitha tutted again.

Lili spun around. "Who cares about competing? As long as there's horses, that's all that matters to me."

Tabitha scowled and continued to put things on her shelf.

Lili grinned at George, causing the dimples in her cheeks to deepen. "So, did you come far today?"

George nodded, remembering how long it had taken.

"Yeah, we set off early this morning. It took ages… How long did it take you?"

"Er… about three days," Lili giggled.

"*Three* days!"

"Lili's from Lekoala," Katie said.

"It's a small island near Fiji," Lili added. "It's beautiful – full of white beaches, forests and mountains, and the horse riding is amazing. You can ride through the sea most of the way round the coast." Her wide brown eyes lit up as she spoke. "And it's certainly much warmer than here."

"It sounds amazing. Do you live there with your parents?"

Lili's smile faltered a moment. "Yeah." She nodded. "Parents, younger brother, the usual. But enough about them!" She quickly changed the subject. "How do you like Paddock Grove so far?"

"It's amazing," George said. "Have you got a horse here too?"

"Yeah, my horse is called Ted." She smiled again and looked across to the photo on her bedside cabinet.

George stared at Ted's picture. If she'd thought

Meg's horse had looked impressive, she was nothing next to Ted: a glorious dapple grey, with delicate curving ears and a gorgeous flowing mane. The kind of horse you'd stop on the street to stare at.

Katie rolled her eyes indulgently at her friend. "Lili's always showing off pictures of Ted. Both me and Lili are on the DIY livery scheme to save money on stabling costs, so we'll be mucking out and feeding our horses the same as you, George. After tomorrow, you'll have to feed Bear in the morning before he's turned out to the field, which Mr Thatcher and the yard staff do. They'll bring in as well during the autumn and spring terms because it gets dark while we're still in class. But if we're riding, we can go and get them ourselves."

"And don't worry, we'll help you – we sometimes take it in turns to feed each other's horses in the mornings," Lili trilled.

George looked at Lili in surprise. Coming from across the world and owning a horse like Ted, George would have thought Lili's parents could afford full livery – but it would be rude to say so.

"We're going to have so much fun!" Lili clapped.

"Not all of us," Tabitha muttered. "I'd like to be able to do DIY."

"Can't you ask your parents to let you?" George asked.

Tabitha glared at her. "Not all of us got to bring our own horse."

George's cheeks burnt. She hadn't meant to put her foot in it.

"Oh, come on, Tabitha, George didn't know," Lili said, skipping around. "If you really want to, you can always help me. In fact, how about you do the freezing mornings, and I can stay in bed!" she giggled.

Tabitha glared. "As you can see, Lili doesn't even care. She never takes anything seriously." She shook her head and didn't say anything else, but George could see she looked upset.

"You'll be able to call home later if you want to." Katie glanced at George. "I only call a couple of times a week, because Mum and Dad are so busy."

"I don't even bother. I'll only get their voicemail," Tabitha said, rolling her eyes.

George felt herself relax a little. She moved towards

her new bed and sat down. She yawned, suddenly feeling tired.

"Don't go to sleep yet – we've still got to unpack our trunks," Katie said, which made Lili groan.

"Anyone fancy unpacking mine for me?" Lili asked hopefully.

"Are you joking?" Tabitha scowled again.

"No… If you do, I'll let you have my ice cream pudding tomorrow."

Tabitha looked at her with wide eyes. "Unpack your trunk for an ice cream pudding? No thanks."

"Oh please," Lili begged and giggled.

"No!"

"What about you, Katie?"

"No, do it yourself. Sometimes you can be so lazy, Lili."

Lili looked at George then. "I don't suppose you—"

"No! George doesn't want to," Katie interrupted before Lili had finished.

"Fine." Lili winked at George. "See how horrible they are to me?"

"Oh, just ignore her, George," Katie said, good-humouredly pretending to put her hand over Lili's face to hide her from view. "But we'd better get on with unpacking. We can't be late for supper, and we're not allowed to miss it – not that I'd want to. It's always so nice!"

"Katie's never met a rule she doesn't follow," Lili said with a mischievous twinkle in her eye. "Don't worry about all the things you can't do here, George. What you really want to know is what you can get away with, right?"

George couldn't help but smile – Lili's playful nature was infectious.

Katie reddened. "There's nothing wrong with following the rules, it's—"

"BORING!" Lili interrupted loudly.

Katie fought back a smile. "*Anyway*, after supper, Mrs Hawksworth will introduce the new house captains."

Lili groaned. "But when that's over, then *we can sleep*." She stood up on her bed, just to fall dramatically back down onto it with a bounce. Immediately seizing the opportunity, Katie grabbed one of her pillows, swinging it round to thump Lili across the middle. A moment later, Tabitha joined in, grabbing another pillow before waving it around her head, roaring with laughter as she launched herself into battle.

"Come on, George, let's see how good you are at a Paddock Grove pillow fight!" Lili shouted with delight.

George didn't hesitate. She snatched up a pillow and rushed over, leaping onto the bed and laughing. And as feathers flew and the girls' giggles echoed around the dorm, George was starting to feel at home at Paddock Grove already.

Chapter Eight

HOOVES ON THE LOOSE

The next morning, pupils streamed through the tall doors of the main hall for the first assembly, the air buzzing with chatter and shuffling feet. As George filed in with the rest of Year Eight, she gazed at the beams that soared above her and the elegant chandeliers hanging from the ceiling.

Sunlight poured through arched windows, their heavy red velvet curtains pulled back. At the front of the hall stood a large raised stage with a polished wooden podium in the middle. Behind it was a large, round stained-glass window of horses running free.

George sat nervously on one of the rows of wooden benches carved with delicate horse designs, fighting back a yawn and trying not to fidget. Everyone else looked much more confident than she felt, which didn't help.

"Are you alright?" Katie, who was sitting next to her, asked.

"I don't know why, but I'm a bit nervous … and a bit tired." The yawn she was fighting broke free. "I'll have to get used to getting up and sorting out Bear before school." Having never had a horse of her own, all George's yard work at the riding school had taken place *after* school, not before. It had felt strange waking up in the still-dark dorm rather than her own bedroom, but it was lovely looking out across the fields through the window next to her bed. Any pang of homesickness disappeared as she chatted away to the other girls, went out to feed Bear, then talked to Mr Thatcher – who told her that Bear wouldn't be turned out this morning until the school's vet had checked him over.

When she'd tentatively asked whether Bear would stay in the stable next to Ophelia, Mr Thatcher had tutted and told her that he was the one who decided where to stable the horses, not the students. She wasn't sure whether he was annoyed with her or with Meg – either way, he seemed very stern.

Everything had taken longer than she'd expected, though. Although they weren't mucking out on the first morning, she'd spilt chaff on the floor of the feed shed, *then* she couldn't find where the yard brushes were stored. She hadn't wanted to ask for help because she'd asked Katie and Lili lots of questions already, so by the time she'd found the brush, she was running late.

After a very quick shower, she'd rushed to put on the green-and-blue tartan kilt, white blouse and grey blazer with the school badge that she needed for classes. She'd fumbled a bit with the green-striped Stroller House tie, not used to knotting one, and the white socks and black lace-up shoes felt uncomfortable and formal compared to the slip-ons that she'd worn to her old school.

George's head was spinning with all the new stuff she had to do, and she ran her hands over the pleats of her skirt to stop them shaking.

"You'll be fine," Katie reassured her as Mrs Hawksworth strode to the podium. The headmistress's steel-wool hair was pulled back in a tight bun, her brown tweed suit immaculate.

The room instantly fell silent.

"Good morning, girls." Mrs Hawksworth's crisp accent rang through the hall. "Welcome to another year at Paddock Grove. Excellence isn't just something we do, but the way we think." She surveyed the room with sharp eyes. "This year, we will strive for greatness in all areas. In riding, as in life, we must always look ahead."

Lili nudged George. "Mrs Hawksworth always likes to start her assemblies dramatically."

"Shhh," Katie hushed her.

"Stop being so boring," Lili tutted. "You can be such a goody-goody."

"I just don't want to get into trouble," Katie whispered defensively.

"What's the big deal?" Lili shook her head and grinned at George.

Suddenly, a giggle erupted from somewhere in the hall. Mrs Hawksworth's eyes narrowed and her gaze darted around, but before she could speak, more giggles followed. Girls were turning in their seats, pointing towards the large windows.

George looked where everyone was pointing, and her stomach dropped to the floor.

Outside on the perfectly manicured lawn was Bear! He was happily munching on a flower bed, petals scattered around him like confetti. Just as Bear had escaped from Albert's sheep shed, *somehow* he'd escaped from Paddock Grove's state-of-the-art stalls. She can't have bolted his stable firmly enough this morning when she'd gone to check on him.

"This is all I need," George whispered, her face burning with embarrassment. She slunk down in her seat, wishing she could disappear.

Mrs Hawksworth's face turned thunderous. She clapped her hands hard. "Silence!" she demanded, her voice sharp and clear. "Students of Paddock Grove, we *do not* abandon decorum at the first sign of disruption. Sit down *now*."

As the girls returned to their seats and the laughter died down, Mrs Hawksworth's eyes scanned the room. They settled on George. "Miss Harris." Her tone was icy and her expression less tolerant than yesterday. "Please stand up."

Katie and Lili gave her sympathetic smiles as George rose to her feet, her legs feeling wobbly. She wanted the ground to open and swallow her up. This was a disaster!

"It seems that once again your pony needs assistance," Mrs Hawksworth stated, her words clipped. "Please attend to him immediately."

"Yes, Mrs Hawksworth," George managed to mumble, before hurrying towards the exit with everyone's eyes following her.

As she headed out, she caught sight of Meg smirking at her.

"Whoops," Meg murmured. "Looks like *someone* should've checked the bolt properly if they wanted to keep that donkey in the stable."

George battled back her tears and, as the door of the grand hall closed behind her, she could hear Mrs Hawksworth resuming her speech. "Discipline is the cornerstone of success, and here at Paddock Grove, from the ground up, we conquer..."

George didn't wait to hear the rest as she raced towards the lawn, wiping her tears away and wondering how on earth she was going to get through the term if Bear kept causing chaos.

Chapter Nine

FIRST-DAY CHALLENGES

In between worrying about whether or not Bear was going to escape again, George spent the morning getting lost. First, she ended up in the Maths class of the year below before realizing she should be in the other teaching block for English. After break, she at least managed to get to the science lab, only to find out that the reason no one looked familiar was because she was in Year Ten GCSE Chemistry. She'd sat at the back of the class before working up the courage to excuse herself while everyone laughed.

She hadn't felt like saying much while she ate lunch with everyone. Now, though, she was changed and ready to ride.

Bear's saddle and bridle were in the tack room, which smelt familiar to her.

George had never seen so many saddles in one place, not even at the saddlery shop near her home. There were dressage saddles, eventing saddles, jumping saddles, general-purpose saddles – there was even a colourful tasselled Western saddle in the far corner.

"Are you excited?" Lili asked as she zipped up her black leather riding boots. George watched as she took Ted's bridle off the hook. She was surprised to see how expensive it looked. It was made of the softest-looking leather and its browband was encrusted with diamante.

"Everyone's looking forward to seeing you ride," Lili added.

George collected her heavy leather saddle with its red numnah from the rack she'd been allocated. Usually, riding in front of people wouldn't worry her at all. In fact, she'd be looking forward to it. But right now, not having ever ridden Bear, and remembering what he was like when she'd watched him at the riding school, she didn't feel very confident. She'd never been like this before. Usually she was the first to want to get in the saddle, but the thought of riding Bear made her feel queasy.

"Try not to worry, George. Bear will be great, I'm sure – you'll be amazing together." Lili offered her a reassuring smile. "Just enjoy it," she said. "That's why you're here, after all. Who cares about anything else?"

George wished she had Lili's carefree approach to everything. Nothing seemed to worry her, although George still wasn't sure why she hadn't been keen on talking about her parents.

"Thank you." George took a deep breath and carried her things out of the tack room.

"See you in the arena," Lili called after her. "Good luck."

George made her way to Bear's stable, taking another deep breath. Perching the numnah, saddle and bridle on one arm, she slipped open the bolt.

"Come on, boy," she said softly, "let's do this, shall we?"

Bear stared at her, looking like he didn't want to have anything to do with riding either and would rather stay in the stable eating his haylage. Carefully, George placed the numnah and saddle on his back, making sure it sat comfortably. She hoped the familiarity of being in a stable and tacking up would help settle her nerves.

Expertly, she tightened the girth, checking it wasn't pinching. She slipped the bridle on him, making sure the loose ring snaffle (that she'd spent hours scrubbing to get rid of the grass stains the night before she left home) slid gently into Bear's mouth without touching his teeth.

Giving the tack one last check-over, George led Bear out, walking him towards one of the entrances to the school's Olympic-size arena, while trying to ignore the creaking of his old tack and the state of his unkempt coat. He really needed to be clipped, but there hadn't been time, and she didn't have clippers of her own anyway. Maybe she could ask to borrow some from the school…

As they entered the enormous arena, George tried to calm her nerves again as she saw a large gathering of girls, some on horses, some watching. Her heart dropped. She'd assumed that the girls who weren't riding would be at lessons, but there were at least fifteen spectating.

The surface was perfect: springy under her feet and stretching out before her, reminding her of some of the competition venues she'd been to. The jumps looked both colourful and exciting, but her heart sank when she spotted Meg and her friends already mounted on their beautiful horses. That was all she needed.

George had never had to worry about sharing lessons with older years at her previous school, and though Katie had said that Paddock Grove had a few mixed year-group lessons, George hadn't realized that meant she would have one with Meg and her horrible friends.

Katie, sitting on Sheriff, gave her an encouraging smile from across the arena.

Ms Stopcroft, the head riding coach, strode into the arena, her polished riding boots gleaming. She wore a fitted navy jacket and crisp white shirt buttoned right up. Her short blonde hair barely moved as she turned her head, sharp blue eyes scanning the mounted riders and the girls watching from the sidelines. But then she smiled, and George saw the warmth in her eyes. She looked young to be the head coach, but George had read in the school brochure about how experienced she was and how often she'd led Paddock Grove's team to victory.

"Alright, everyone," she called out, her voice clear and firm. "Eyes on me, please. Let's break up into groups for a warm-up, and then we can do some individual rounds."

The chatter died down immediately. Even the horses seemed to stand a little straighter as Ms Stopcroft spoke. "As you know, girls, we'll be considering our team for next term's inter-school championships over the coming weeks," she announced. Her gaze swept over the group again, staying for a moment on each rider in turn. "This is your chance to start showing me what you're made of, so do yourself proud and you'll do me proud too." She smiled warmly, then she paced along the line of mounted girls. "As always, I want you to ride well, ride safely, ride kindly and ride to win. Those are the qualities I'll be looking for in our team, and, although we're often competing against one another, that doesn't mean we shouldn't show respect at all times."

George listened with growing anxiety as Ms Stopcroft divided them into three groups of five for warm-up. Each group would then be called over to the far end of the arena where some girls having their stable management lesson were setting up practice jumps to "put everyone through their paces".

Absent-mindedly, George looked around and caught sight of Meg rolling her eyes at Jessica, who was riding a beautiful grey pony. They grinned, and George turned away when they spotted her looking at them.

"Everything alright, George?" Ms Stopcroft walked across to where George and Bear were standing. George wanted to say that nothing was alright, not the saddle, not the bridle, not Bear and not the fact that she didn't have Timmy, but instead she just nodded.

She pulled down her stirrups on the saddle as Ms Stopcroft stood watching her.

"I'm pleased to have you at Paddock Grove, George. The moment I saw you on horseback, I knew you were a gifted rider."

George could only just manage to muster a quiet "*Thank you*". She felt positively ill. In her heart she knew it was nerves, but what if she couldn't live up to Ms Stopcroft's expectations? What if she made a fool of herself in front of everyone? What if she let everyone down?

"Hop on, then," Ms Stopcroft encouraged her, smiling.

With trembling hands, George pulled on her riding gloves, checked her hat strap was secure and gathered her reins. Putting her foot in the stirrup and with the help of Ms Stopcroft giving her a leg up, George swung herself into the saddle.

This was the first time she'd sat on Bear, and she took a deep breath. He felt so different to Timmy. For a start, he was smaller and much, much broader.

"When you're ready, take him down the long side and warm him up with your group. I'll call you across when it's your turn," Ms Stopcroft said, breaking George's thoughts.

From the corner of her eye, George caught sight of the two other groups. Everyone looked fantastic, jumping with ease and looking like they were enjoying themselves. She took another deep breath. She had to keep telling herself she could do this. She knew how to ride … so why was she feeling so shaky?

Checking the girth one last time and pulling it one hole tighter, George watched Ms Stopcroft walk away, then squeezed her legs on Bear. He didn't budge. "Come on, Bear," she encouraged him. "Bear, come on." She squeezed again, but, unbothered by the movement, Bear happily gazed around. "Bear, *please*, don't do this to me."

Embarrassment crept over George. She looked up and saw Meg smirking.

"Bear!" George hissed under her breath. The last thing she wanted was to let on that Bear wouldn't even move!

As she was about to completely despair, Bear suddenly decided to move, and George let out a sigh of relief. She was pleasantly surprised to feel how forward he was. Although his movements were choppy, he was powerful – the strength coming from his hind legs.

George let herself glance over again to the other groups. It would be her turn soon. The problem was, she had no idea what would happen. Would Bear do as she asked or not?

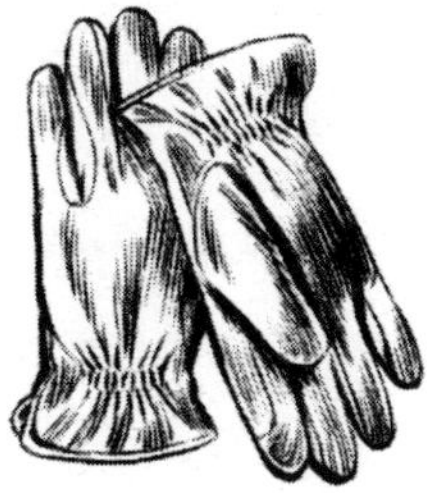

Chapter Ten

SPOTLIGHT IN THE ARENA

"Group three, can you come over?"

George had been warming up in the same group as Meg, who – other than smirking – hadn't said much so far, but George couldn't imagine that lasting.

"Group three!" Ms Stopcroft's voice floated across the arena and George turned to see that the other two groups had finished, which meant one thing: all eyes were on *her* group.

The pressure of the moment hung in the air, thick and heavy, and George licked her dry lips and swallowed hard, trying to look confident as she nodded to Ms Stopcroft.

"Now, I want to introduce you to our newcomer,

Georgia Harris," Ms Stopcroft said. "We're very lucky to have her join Paddock Grove."

George saw the girls look at her.

"I'm sure a lot of you can learn from her. Her riding test to get into the school was nothing less than exceptional." With a nod towards George, she said, "Let's begin. Miss Harris – George – why don't you go first? Show us what you can do."

It was time.

For better or for worse, George was about to show Paddock Grove what she was made of. Positioning herself in the saddle, she decided it was best to keep her focus in front of her rather than look across at all the girls. She wished her group had gone first so she didn't have both other groups watching her. Pushing everything out of her mind, she guided Bear into a more balanced trot. Then she helped him by keeping him out on the left rein to stop him falling in so much.

As she continued around the arena, George felt him relaxing, making his trot much smoother. "That's it, Bear."

She watched his ear twist back as he listened to her talk.

"Now at the halfway mark, I'd like you to pick up a canter, then aim for the red crossbar," Ms Stopcroft called.

George changed the position of her leg, asking Bear to move into a canter. For a moment, it felt perfect, and a smile spread across her face. "That's it, Bear," she urged him again, as a spark of hope rose in her.

Excited, she turned Bear towards the jump. As he moved off, his hooves thudding softly on the arena surface, George concentrated on keeping her hands steady. They approached the jump, a simple cross-pole, and George lined Bear up, looking between his pricked ears at the poles ahead.

"Keep your leg on!" Ms Stopcroft shouted. "Keep driving him forward."

George's excitement grew as they got closer.

Three strides away … two … one … and …

Bear hesitated.

Without warning, he lowered his neck and skidded to a halt, planting his feet. The abrupt stop sent George tumbling over his neck, and she landed with a thud on the arena surface.

Uninjured, but thoroughly embarrassed, George sat up and battled back tears. She felt cross with Bear. She *knew* he would be hopeless, and now he'd made her look stupid in front of everyone!

Ms Stopcroft hurried over. "George, are you alright?"

"Yes, thank you… I'm not hurt." *Except for my ego!*

Ms Stopcroft lowered her voice. "Try not to let nerves get the better of you. I know it's hard to perform in front of everyone, but you're a fantastic rider – that's why you got the place here." She smiled and held out her hand to help George up. "Ready to try again?"

George nodded and dusted the sand off her jodhpurs. Keeping her eyes on the ground, she accepted another leg up by Ms Stopcroft.

"I thought she was supposed to be able to ride." Tabitha's voice carried across the arena. *"Even having to ride a school horse, I think my place on the team is safe."*

"Be quiet," Lili snapped at Tabitha. But George had heard. Miserably, she pulled herself back into the saddle.

Bear shifted uneasily beneath her, mirroring her own worries. She patted his neck, trying not to be frustrated with him, but she couldn't help feeling resentful. This would never have happened with her beloved Timmy. She'd be holding her head up high now. She couldn't recall a single time that Timmy had refused a jump, no matter how daunting.

Then, trying to muster up some confidence, George murmured, "Let's try this again, shall we?"

As they broke into a trot and then a canter, Ms Stopcroft's voice rang out. "Half halt, George! Keep him balanced! Help him out. Don't let him snatch the reins. Shoulders down, sit up, keep your hands still... That's it, drive him on."

George aimed for the jump again, a jump she would usually clear with her eyes closed. "Go on, Bear, go on." She urged him on, but she could tell the moment before he did it that Bear was going to dig his heels in. Sure enough, just like before, he planted and George flew forward, but this time she was ready and clung onto Bear's neck to avoid falling off.

As she straightened up, she heard Meg's laughter ringing across the arena. George ignored her as she aimed Bear for another jump. He cantered towards it smoothly, but just as George thought that they were going to jump it, Bear suddenly swerved to the side of the jump wing, and it was all George could do to hang on.

She steadied herself in the saddle. Tears of humiliation clouded her vision.

"Your turn now, Meg. Aim for the cross-pole, then continue with the course." George was certain she could hear frustration in Ms Stopcroft's voice. She'd let everyone down, and now George felt wretched.

Hearing the thud of hooves approaching, George glanced up and saw Meg, perched elegantly on Ophelia, cantering past. Ophelia moved with effortless grace, her muscles rippling.

As Meg guided Ophelia towards the double, her posture was perfect. Approaching it, Ophelia's ears pricked forward and her stride began to lengthen. Then, in a burst of graceful force, she launched into the air, her powerful legs tucked neatly beneath her. For a split second, both Ophelia and Meg seemed to glide like a feather through the air, then they landed with ease on the other side, moving beautifully into the next magnificent stride.

Meg and Ophelia continued around the course,

each jump higher than the last. As they soared over the last jump, landing smoothly on the other side, applause broke out from the watching students.

Meg trotted Ophelia over to where George was on Bear.

"That's how it's supposed to be done... Maybe you should tell your donkey that, or maybe you should realize there's no place here for someone who can't ride." With a flick of her reins, and her nose pointed up in the air, Meg trotted back to the middle to join the others.

After the last three in George's group had finished their round, Ms Stopcroft called the names of girls to stay behind to try the harder jumps. George's name wasn't on the list.

As George jumped off Bear and began to lead him out of the arena, she hoped that the brim of her hat would be enough to hide her tears.

"George... George!"

George glanced up and saw Katie ride over on Sheriff.

"Whatever Meg said, ignore her, George. It doesn't matter what she thinks."

George shook her head, fighting very hard to stop any more tears. She was so embarrassed. It felt like Bear had done nothing but show her up in front of everyone.

"She's right, though," George muttered. "Maybe I don't belong here. I can't even get Bear over a tiny jump."

"That's not true," Katie insisted. "You just need to get to know Bear better. You and Bear need to be a team… It'll come, I promise."

"Katie, I didn't tell you to have a natter on the way round," Ms Stopcroft shouted (not unkindly).

"Sorry, Ms Stopcroft," Katie called, then she brought her voice back down. "I better go." She moved Sheriff into a working trot as George nodded, grateful for her support. She sighed, wondering if she'd ever fit in at Paddock Grove.

Chapter Eleven

AFTER-SCHOOL FUN

The September evening was warm as George and Bear trudged towards the old oak tree near the school's cross-country course. She'd had a little bit of time to think, and the more she thought, the more upset she felt; and the more upset she felt, the more she missed home. Everything was a disaster. The first week at Paddock Grove had been totally miserable for her. Dreams of joining the advanced riding group had been crushed when Ms Stopcroft had placed her in the lower group, focusing solely on flatwork and endless trotting poles.

George found this utterly humiliating – not to mention that it was a great source of amusement for Meg and her friends. Thankfully she could avoid them most of the time as they were in the year above, and in another house. When she did see them, though, Meg was always quick with a nasty comment. Even though they were older, they seemed to delight in being mean. Katie told George to ignore them, but that was easier said than done. What made the whole situation worse, was that each day she had to watch Katie and Lili in the main arena, jumping courses and in the running to be picked for the inter-school and regional competitions. It was everything she knew she was capable of and should be doing.

Her longing for Timmy and her daily resentment had been growing. Now she could barely look at Bear and rushed through stable duties.

"Hi!" She tried to sound cheerful as she waved to Katie and Lili, who were already waiting, perched on the gnarled roots that poked out of the ground. The two of them had been so kind that despite everything George found it hard to be jealous, and after seeing her so sad, they'd invited her to the cross-country course to help her practise. At first, she'd refused, but Katie had told her how she used to come and practise with Sheriff when she was struggling with him. It was the perfect place because no one was around.

Even though George felt down in the dumps, it was still wonderful to be here. The sprawling grounds of Paddock Grove stretched out before her, lush green fields and dense woods surrounded them, and in the distance the grand stone buildings of the school stood proudly against the sky.

George tied Bear to the one of the several tie posts dotted around the edges of the cross-country course and the beginning of the bridle path that led through the woods.

She slumped down next to her friends, her frustration from the day's riding lesson still bothering her. "I want to get rid of Bear," she blurted out, her voice cracking slightly. "I'm going to speak to Mum and Dad later. Then at least I'll be able to use one of the school's horses."

Katie's eyes widened in shock. "George! Don't say that." Katie began to make a fuss of Bear, which made George feel guilty. She knew she hadn't given him the attention that she used to give Timmy. "Maybe Bear's picking up on how you feel about him. Horses are sensitive, you know."

George pulled a face. "Not Bear – the only thing he's sensitive to is where his next meal is." As if to prove her point, Bear nudged her pocket looking for a treat. "He's nothing like Timmy." Her voice broke. She didn't want to think about Timmy, but it was impossible. "Bear is useless," George said dramatically. She knew that wasn't quite true, but she felt miserable.

"That's not true," Katie said. "He's going so much better in lessons. You just don't know him yet, and some horses need more help than others. I have to practise *all the time* on Sheriff. He's a great all-rounder, but to get even close to being on the teams we have to do extra work, especially when it comes to cross-country. That's why we came out here to practise. Not like Lili with Ted. Ted is just amazing." George saw the pride on Katie's face as she spoke about Lili. "Like, really amazing. He's probably the best horse here."

George nodded. She'd only seen Lili ride him once, but she could tell how incredible Ted was. Ted was certainly the sort of horse she saw on posters.

Lili smiled proudly. "Yeah, but I don't do cross-country. I'm too worried he might injure himself."

"Are your parents horsey too?" George asked.

Again, Lili's smile changed at the mention of her parents, this time flaring false and bright as she laughed off the question with, "Oh no, no, not horsey at all! But yes, Katie's right about Bear..." She fiddled with the strap of her sparkling gold riding hat, which was sitting on her lap, and changed the subject. "You have to give Bear more time. Think about it – you're probably riding him like you would've ridden Timmy. You need to get used to his movements." She looked up and found her real, warm smile once more. "It's like... OK, it's like dancing with someone new. You can't expect to know all the steps right away."

Lili got up and started to whirl around, giggling, and Katie frowned. "Be serious, Lili."

"I am. I'm just showing George how she needs to dance with Bear." Lili continued to whirl about. "That's all you need to do, George – learn his dance."

George sighed, twisting a blade of grass between her fingers. "I guess. But ... but how am I supposed to get on the team if I can't even get him over a tiny jump? I know I can do it... I know I can, but not on Bear.

I still think I should at least *see* if I could ride one of the school's horses. Maybe that way I'll at least have a chance. Everyone's talking about the selection, and I don't want to miss out."

"You can still make the team. Mrs Hawksworth and Ms Stopcroft don't decide who's in until much later in the term." Katie's eyes lit up warmly. "But if you don't try with Bear, why should he try with you? It goes both ways, you know."

George nodded slowly, knowing there was truth to Katie's words. She hadn't been trying – even Albert had picked that up. *If you want to build a bond with him, you've got to do more than just feed and water him*, he'd said to her; and she knew he was right. Not only did she barely look at Bear, George had spent no more time in the stable with him than necessary. But that didn't stop her frustration at still feeling like she couldn't ride.

Lili suddenly stopped spinning and stared at her. "Hey, I've got an idea. Can I have a go on Bear? Maybe I can show you what I mean."

George looked at her friend in surprise. "Of course you can!"

Although she didn't know why Lili would want to. The rumour she'd heard about Ted was that he was one of the most expensive horses at Paddock Grove. It was a puzzle that Lili's unhorsey parents had bought such a valuable horse and then put her through school on a DIY livery package. Maybe they'd spent so much money on Ted that this was the only way they could afford the fee? Whatever the reason, George was grateful that no one else in her year had taken the single scholarship slot that she'd been offered. Her parents could only afford for her to have Bear *because* he would be stabled here during term time with the costs covered by the company sponsoring her scholarship.

The little cottage George's family lived in probably wasn't worth as much as Ted. George pushed these thoughts aside, focusing instead on watching Lili prepare to ride Bear.

Once she had put on her hat, Lili mounted him unaided. "Come on, boy, let's show them how special you really are." Speaking softly to Bear, Lili gave a click of the tongue and settled in the saddle.

George watched curiously as Lili began to ride him.

She couldn't believe it. It was like watching a different pony. Bear had his ears pricked up and he responded to the barest of squeezes from Lili. When he made a grab for the long grass, Lili caught him with a firm, "Later, Bear."

She guided Bear through the different gaits, her body moving in perfect time with his. She adapted to his short, strong trot, which George knew was a world away from Ted's beautiful long strides. Then, when Lili took him into canter, she sat deeply in her seat, and George was amazed when Bear took off on the right leg and was guided by Lili into a perfect figure of eight. Why wouldn't he do that for her? All he'd done is try and dump her at every jump possible.

"See that?" Katie spoke quietly. "Lili's feeling Bear's movements … reading him. She's a superb rider. I have to think through every step, but Lili just … well, she just gets it, you know? It's like she can read the horses' minds or something."

Lili aimed Bear at a low brush fence. They cleared it effortlessly, then she popped him over a half tree trunk. Bear's ears were pricked forward, his head up and

George smiled in delight at seeing him enjoy himself like this.

"That was amazing!" Katie said.

The two of them continued to watch Lili, George in awe at how different Bear looked with her. Maybe there was hope after all. Maybe with a lot of practice she and Bear had a chance.

When Lili returned, she was grinning from ear to ear. "George, he's brilliant! He really is. All Bear needs is understanding and a bit of help from you. He needs you to have patience with him. This is all new to him too, you know."

George felt a pang of guilt as she stroked Bear's velvety nose. "Good boy. You were plucky out there. You made that look easy." Seeing Lili ride him like that forced George to admit that maybe this was as much about her as it was about Bear, though that didn't help her feel close to him the way she'd been with Timmy.

"The most important thing," Lili said, dismounting, "is not to let him feel how disappointed you are in him. *We* know you miss Timmy, but that's not Bear's fault. Horses pick up on that stuff. Let him be your champion, and he'll be yours. Trust me." Lili grinned at George. "Now you have a go."

George hesitated, then nodded. She pulled on her hat and leapt up on Bear, settling herself into the saddle.

Taking a deep breath, she closed her eyes for a moment, pushing all thoughts of Timmy and the pressures of Paddock Grove out of her head. She would focus only on Bear. George opened her eyes again and nudged Bear into a walk. "Come on, Bear." And, like Lili, she clicked her tongue.

George sat deep in her seat and concentrated on his movements: the way his back swayed; how his head bobbed slightly with each step. Then they moved up into a trot. Instead of expecting Bear to do all the work, George helped him by adjusting her seat, making her hands light and buttery, and giving him more rein. Timmy had liked a short rein, but she needed to ride Bear differently.

When they broke into a canter, George smiled with a sudden rush of excitement. "That's it, Bear, good boy."

From the corner of her eye, she saw Lili and Katie beaming at her.

Deciding to start small, George aimed for the small log. The closer they got, the more George could feel Bear moving forward. She had to trust him, and she gave Bear his head, allowing him to find his stride.

There was no hesitation this time.

They pushed off, Bear tucking his legs underneath, and George caught her breath and took in the moment. This was the best feeling: the feeling of flying … soaring. Then – too quickly – it was over and they landed, Bear's hooves meeting the ground with a satisfying thud.

George punched the air in delight and patted his neck. "Yes! Clever boy, Bear! You did it! *You did it!*"

For the next fifteen minutes, George and Bear tackled jump after jump. Bear clipped the brush jump with his back hooves a few times, had a small spook at a leaf falling from the oak tree and stumbled slightly as he rounded the corner towards the coffin jump, but instead of George getting frustrated, she spoke to him softly and tried again. As they cleared the final fence, a log pile, which he soared over with great joy and ease, George felt a rush of pride. Lili had been right: she just needed to try harder with Bear.

George patted Bear some more, feeling the slight dampness of his sweat. For the first time since coming to Paddock Grove, she felt some hope. The two of them had a lot of work to do, but maybe, just maybe, she and Bear could make this work after all.

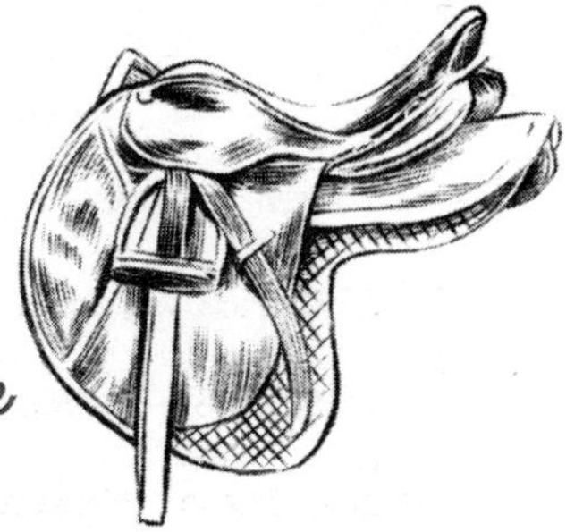

Chapter Twelve

THE RUN-IN

That evening the dormitory was quiet, apart from the occasional rustle of turning pages. George lay on her bed, propped up on her elbows as she flipped through a horse care manual. Working at the riding school certainly hadn't been the same as owning your own horse and now she had a whole new perspective on it.

Katie and Lili were sprawled on the thick rug in the centre of the room, surrounded by textbooks, while Tabitha sat at her desk, drawing.

"This is so boring. I hate Biology. I didn't think we were supposed to have any work to do in the first couple of weeks of term." Lili threw the Biology book in her bag. "I can't be bothered."

Katie glanced at her. "Mrs Daykin said we needed

to swot up before next week's lesson."

Lili grabbed the textbook Katie was holding out of her hands. "It's only for a stupid test. Who cares if we don't get a good mark?"

Katie became serious. "I care, and my parents certainly do."

Lili rolled her eyes.

"If I don't get good marks in science, how am I supposed to become a vet?"

Lili shook her head. "That's ages away – some pointless Biology test won't make any difference."

"Having good school reports will help to get into the best universities. You've got to think about the future. That's what my dad always says."

"Has anyone told you, you can be really boring?" Lili said with an exaggerated yawn.

Katie went red, and George and Tabitha exchanged glances as if they were watching a tennis match – one George certainly wanted to avoid.

"All I want to do with my future is ride horses. That's it," Lili said, getting up and walking towards the window.

"But you'll need to get a job."

"A job will just get in the way." She shrugged. "I'm never going to work." Lili started to skip around. "Never, ever, ever."

Tabitha tutted. "I'm trying to concentrate. Stop being so noisy, Lili."

"You're only drawing," Lili said as she shut the window.

"I like drawing," Tabitha snapped. George had seen the drawings of horses she'd done. They were very good.

"No one needs quiet to draw."

"Well, I don't want to have to do it with your racket… And don't close the window. I want it open."

"It's too cold in here," Lili said, crossing her arms.

"Then put a jumper on." Tabitha glared at her angrily. George actually agreed with Tabitha, but she thought it better not to say anything.

"You take yours off." Lili shrugged again.

Just as it looked like Tabitha and Lili were going to dig in for a long fight about the window, the door swung open with a bang.

Meg stormed in, her face screwed up in anger, along

with her friend Jessica, whose hair didn't seem to have a strand out of place, despite the dramatic entrance. As ever, the older girls brought with them an air of confidence that George found instantly intimidating.

"Is it true?" Meg demanded, her voice shrill. "Are they really going to put that scruffy donkey of yours in a paddock with Ophelia?"

George sat up, her book forgotten. "Don't call him a donkey. His name's Bear."

"A big, hairy Bear." Meg grinned nastily.

"Stop saying that." George's voice was stronger this time.

Meg blinked. "Er … so what is he then?"

"You know exactly what he is, Meg." Katie stood up. "Stop being so mean. He's George's pony, and he's lovely… Anyway, why are you this side of the school? Shouldn't you be in your own house?"

"I'll go where I want to," Meg said haughtily.

"I'm sure Mrs Hawksworth won't see it like that when she catches you in here."

After supper, all the girls had to go to their own houses. Meg and her friends were in Frankel House – the house with the most wins in the last decade, because *of course* someone like Meg belonged in the winners' house.

"Look," Jessica said as she stepped forward, her dark eyes flashing. "We came here to see if it was true. Ophelia shouldn't be with Bear."

Lili chipped in. "Why not?"

"Why not? *Why not?*" Meg put her hands on her chest. "Because Ophelia is a *very* expensive horse – something George probably wouldn't understand. She's a *horse*: a purebred Trakehner that shouldn't be anywhere near that … that … that cart horse."

"There's nothing wrong with Bear. I wouldn't have a problem with Ted sharing a field with him, so why would you care if Ophelia is in the same field?" Lili said firmly.

Meg ignored her and turned to George again. "You have to go and tell Mrs Hawksworth you don't want this," she insisted.

"It's not up to us who shares paddocks," Katie snapped.

Tabitha shrugged. "I don't see why George can't ask if Meg's so bothered about it."

"Oh, be quiet, Tabitha." Lili scowled. "You're only

saying that because I wouldn't open the window."

"Well, George?" said Meg. "Are you going to say something to Mrs Hawksworth or not?"

George felt everyone's gaze on her. She took a deep breath and, to her own surprise said, "*No*, no I'm not. And please stop calling Bear names. He has as much right to be here as Ophelia."

"George has earnt her place here," Lili said, staring hard at Meg.

Meg and Jessica burst into mean laughter.

"I've yet to see what the fuss is about," Jessica said nastily.

"She can't even get that lump over the lowest of crossbars," Meg added.

"You're just worried that George is such a good rider it wouldn't matter if she really *did* ride a donkey – they'd still make the team before you and your latest ride on the carousel of competition horses that Daddy buys you," Tabitha said.

A silence fell, and Tabitha looked at them all. "What?" She shrugged and went back to her drawing.

Jessica linked arms with Meg. "Come on, you'll

just have to get your father to complain. Let's see what happens then."

And with one last glare, they stormed out, slamming the door behind them.

For a moment, the room was silent again. Then Katie started to giggle. Lili joined in, and soon even George was laughing. All except for Tabitha, they fell about, clutching their sides.

"Girls, what's all this noise?" The housemistress Mrs Winters walked in with a large frown.

"Sorry, Mrs Winters," Katie said straight away.

She gave a small nod. "Well, keep it down, please – and that goes for you too, Lili."

"Yes, Mrs Winters," Lili said as the housemistress walked out of the door, but the moment she had, Lili burst into fits of giggles again.

George grinned, but it didn't stop her wondering why Tabitha always blew hot and cold, and why Lili didn't want to talk about her parents. There was certainly a lot more to learn about her new friends.

Chapter Thirteen

A WHOLE LOT OF WORRY

The vast library of Paddock Grove stretched out before George, its towering shelves filled with books reaching from the shiny floor to the high ceiling above. The scent of polish hung heavy in the air and the afternoon sunlight streamed through the tall arched windows, casting long shadows across the room.

George sat alone at one of the long wooden tables near a window, her Maths textbook open in front of her. After the last class, Lili and Katie had wanted her to go to the stables to look at the new numnahs that had arrived in the post today for Lili and Ted, but she'd made her excuses, saying that she needed to swot up on her Maths.

Large tears fell silently onto the pages of her textbook. Although she loved so much about being at Paddock Grove, when she'd woken up this morning, she'd felt very homesick. Lying in her bed in the shared dorm made her think of her cosy bedroom back home in the little cottage. She missed her mum and dad terribly, and even though she was making great friends, she longed for some of her mum's hugs and for the way her dad still held her hand when they walked to the village shops (when she let him). She even missed Albert, and his rickety old farm, which seemed like a distant, cherished memory.

As another tear splashed onto her book, George tried to stifle a sob. She didn't want anyone to see her crying, especially not the older girls over in the corner.

"George?"

At hearing someone calling her name, she hastily wiped her eyes, hoping whoever it was wouldn't notice she'd been crying. She looked up and saw Tabitha, who was wearing her shirt untucked from her skirt and her tie a little loose.

"Are you alright?" Tabitha asked, sitting down opposite George.

George opened her mouth to make an excuse, but the words wouldn't come. Finally, she managed to whisper, "I'm just really missing home."

"It gets easier," Tabitha said after a pause. "A lot of us get homesick. I'm sorry you're missing home, though."

George nodded gratefully. She took a deep breath, trying to compose herself. "Did you? Did you ever get homesick?"

Tabitha's gaze drifted to the window. "Not really," she replied after a moment. "I've been at boarding school since I was six. I went to Meadowdale, then I came here."

George's eyes widened in shock. "Six?" she gasped. "But that's so young!"

Tabitha shrugged, her face full of hurt. "My parents were too busy to look after me, I guess. They're racehorse trainers, always travelling the world. I've got two brothers who are much older than me, and they're in the racing world too, so I don't see much of my family. Even during holidays, they're rarely home. Sometimes I stay with a school guardian." George gave a sympathetic smile, which seemed to make Tabitha ruffle somewhat. "It's not so bad."

George tried to imagine spending so much time away from her own parents. It would be awful. Even now, George was counting down the days till she'd next see her mum and dad. Messaging just wasn't the same.

A moment of silence stretched between them, but then Tabitha gave George a sad smile. "I know Bear isn't the kind of pony you wanted to bring with you, but you're really lucky that your parents support you and wanted you to have your own horse." Tabitha's eyes suddenly filled with tears and a faraway look came into them. "I used to have a horse here."

"Really?"

Tabitha let out a big sigh. "Her name was Petra. She was my best friend. She was gorgeous – a beautiful midnight-black horse, and she had this white star over her right eye. She was from a great bloodline."

George tried to picture Petra. "What happened to her?"

"She tore her tendon, so she needed to be turned away for a while, but my parents…" She took another deep breath. "When I got back home from term, they'd sent her away to become a broodmare."

George's heart went out to Tabitha. "Couldn't they have kept her?"

Tabitha nodded, then shrugged. "For them, horses are just business. Petra was worth more as a broodmare than she was being mine."

George thought of her own parents, who had scraped and saved to buy Bear and supported her dreams even when it meant sacrifice. "I'm so sorry. Have you got a picture of her?"

"Yes, I'll show you later. She's on my phone. I couldn't bear to have a photo on my bedside – it would've made me too sad." Tabitha blinked rapidly, then in an instant she sat up in her chair and put on a brave face. "Anyway, it's fine, and you'll get used to being away from home. Before you know it, you won't be thinking about it at all."

George nodded and grabbed her books. "Thanks, Tabitha."

"For what?" Tabitha looked puzzled.

"For being kind." She thought of Bear, probably

munching away on the grass, and smiled slightly. At least she had one small piece of home here with her.

But Tabitha wasn't listening, too distracted by one of the newspapers that someone had left out on one of the reading chairs by the window.

"Hey, look at this!" she said, grabbing it to read aloud. *"Horse thieves strike Willowbrook stables..."* She looked up in alarm. "Willowbrook's the village just down the road from here!"

"What does it say?" George asked, crowding in.

"Last night, criminals broke into Willowbrook Riding School and made off with one of their beloved show jumpers. The theft was discovered early yesterday morning when staff arrived to feed the horses. The CCTV had been tampered with. Police are investigating but have no leads so far. Stable owner Mandy Hodges said, 'We're devastated. Our horses are like our family.' Local horse owners are urged to be vigilant."

Tabitha looked up from the paper. "Can you imagine? Someone just walking off with a horse in the middle of the night?"

"That would be terrible."

The two of them packed up their things and headed out of the library and down the corridor together. Tabitha peeled away with a "See you later, George" as they passed the school office, where she had been asked to go and sign some forms.

George watched her go, then she made her way down the busy corridor full of girls.

She felt better after the chat with Tabitha, and she made her way out of the main school and down the path, wandering along the track to Bear's paddock. Despite Meg's protests, Mrs Hawksworth had insisted that Bear and Ophelia share a paddock and, apart from the odd squeal now and then, they seemed to get on well. Usually, Mr Thatcher and his staff would bring the horses in, but George wanted to bring Bear in herself today, especially after what Tabitha had said. It made her think about how she'd been treating him. Since the extra-curricular session at the cross-country course, she and Bear had been getting along much better in lessons, but what Tabitha had said about Petra had got George thinking. Bear wasn't just a horse to ride in lessons; he was *her* horse.

As George approached the paddock, she frowned.

"Bear?" she called out, her gaze wandering towards the trees. There was no sign of Bear or Ophelia.

"Bear!"

George hurried over, and when she reached the fence, she saw a section of the wooden rail broken, with splintered wood scattered on the grass.

"Oh no," George groaned. Bear had clearly done his escape trick again, but this time he'd taken Ophelia with him.

Just then, George heard footsteps behind her. She whirled round and saw Meg walking towards the paddock with a diamante head collar in her hand.

Meg stared into the deserted paddock. "Where's Ophelia? What have you done with her? I said, where is she?" The panic on Meg's face was quickly replaced by anger.

George shook her head. "I – I don't know. I came to get Bear, and I saw the fence broken... They can't have got far."

Meg's eyes widened as she saw the broken fence George was talking about. "This is all your fault! I told Mrs Hawksworth it was a bad idea, and look what's happened… Ophelia! *Ophelia!*" She shouted for her, striding into the field and looking around.

"Come on, we need to go and find them," George said, trying to keep her voice steady and not panic.

Meg stared at her. "I'm not going anywhere with *you*." She pulled out her phone from the pocket on the side of her jodhpurs. "Jess and Harriet will help."

George didn't bother replying and began to run, searching for Bear. But without the map in the information pack, George realized she still didn't know the grounds well enough. Well, Meg wasn't the only one who could call her friends…

Within minutes, Katie and Lili came running up the path. They were dressed in their jodhpurs and riding hoodies, and their faces were flushed.

Slightly out of breath, Lili came to a stop in front of her. "George, try not to worry. We'll find him."

Katie gave her a small smile. "We will."

The girls split up, each taking a different direction to search the vast grounds, with George searching the fields closest to the stables, worried that it wasn't just Bear who would end up lost.

After twenty minutes, which felt more like hours, George heard Lili's excited shout from a distant field. "I found them! *I found them*... We're over here!"

George raced towards the sound of Lili's voice, charging up the steep hill. At the top, by the hedges, Bear and Ophelia grazed contentedly side by side.

"Bear!" George let out a loud sigh of relief, but once again felt a twinge of frustration. Why couldn't Bear just behave? Why did he always have to be so naughty? But then he lifted his head and looked at her with big, soft eyes. She sighed again. She hadn't thought Bear would care if she was here or not.

"Ophelia!" Meg and Jessica charged past George before Meg ran her hands over her horse, checking for any signs of injury. "Are you OK? What did that ... that" – Meg paused to turn to Bear – "that awful *thing* do to you?"

"Bear didn't do anything to her. They both look happy," George said indignantly.

"Happy?" Meg waved her arms around. "Does she look *happy* to you?"

"She does, actually." Katie patted Bear and looked

at Ophelia, who was ignoring Meg's melodrama and nibbling happily on the grass.

"I agree." Lili smiled at Meg, who scowled back.

Bear nudged George with his big, heavy head and nibbled at the hem of her coat. It made her smile.

Meg rounded on her. "Your pony is a terrible influence, George! He could have got Ophelia seriously hurt. What if they'd wandered onto the road?"

"The nearest road is a very long way from here and hardly any traffic uses it," sighed Lili.

Just then, Meg's other friend, Harriet, arrived. She was in the same year as George but a different form. The only lesson they had together was PE, when Harriet spent her time making fun of George because she'd never played hockey before. "Is Ophelia alright?" She peered at Bear with disdain. Her short hair was poker straight, and her nose curled up in disgust. "That scruffy thing caused all this trouble?"

Lili stepped forward, her eyes flashing as fierce as a thunderstorm. "They're both *fine*, and no one was there when it happened, so it might well have been Ophelia who broke out, not Bear."

Meg stared at her, then shook her head. "As if."

Tutting, she slipped on Ophelia's sparkly head collar, clipped the red rope on it and marched away, Ophelia looking disappointed at being dragged off the lush grass.

George sighed again. Like Meg, she clipped a lead rope to Bear's field-safety head collar, which Mr Thatcher had given him the other day, after his staff complained that Bear didn't want to be caught when they tried to bring him in. "Come on, you – let's get you back in the stable."

As they walked over, Lili fell into step with George. "You know," she said with a grin, "I think Bear quite liked breaking out and taking Ophelia with him. He probably knew what Meg would say."

They all laughed and continued to chatter as they made their way back to the yard, where George spotted a tall Black girl with her afro hair tied up in bunches.

"Hi, everyone." The girl waved, and her striking brown eyes twinkled. She wore a tailored cream riding jacket and white jodhpurs.

"Misty!" Katie shrieked with delight. "When did you get back?"

"About half an hour ago. I flew in from the junior championships in France. Dream was amazing… We managed to get placed. I'm so proud of her."

Misty nodded towards her horse, who stood patiently outside her stable. She was a palomino with a white blaze running down her face, and George thought her coat looked like it had been spun from gold.

"I've missed you all. The summer holidays seemed so long. I'm so pleased to be back at Paddock Grove," Misty continued, her French accent tripping off her words.

"I've missed you too." Lili skipped towards her.

"And I hear I've missed some excitement," Misty added. "Harriet told me all about it."

Katie shook her head. "I hope she didn't tell you it was Bear's fault… Oh, this is George – the new girl Mrs Hawksworth told us about."

Misty turned to look at George, who was standing with Bear. "So you're going to be our secret superpower, are you?"

George looked puzzled. "What do you mean?"

Misty smiled and walked over to stroke Bear's nose.

"Ms Stopcroft is always on the look out for riders to

represent the school in competitions. We don't want it to only be Frankel students who make the team do we?" Her eyes twinkled as she looked at George.

"The youth eventing challenge is due to take place after half term. So, with your showjumping skills," Misty continued, "my dressage skills, and if we all start practising now… What do you say? A hundred per cent Stroller House team?"

George's eyes widened. "An actual competition? Already?" She chewed on her lip nervously.

"It's fantastic, isn't it?"

George wasn't so sure. "I don't know if I'd call myself a superpower," she said apologetically.

Misty smiled. "What do you think, Bear?" She stroked him again. "Are you ready to show the everyone what you can do? I'm certain between us all we can show them what we're really made of."

The other girls cheered as George looked at Bear. The problem was, *she* wasn't sure if she was ready. Even though George tried hard not to, she found herself longing again for Timmy…

Chapter Fourteen

BEAR'S UPSET

Over the next few days, George continued to practise. She was still stuck in the lower riding classes, while the others were riding at a much more advanced level. She certainly hoped that today's riding practice would be better than yesterday's session, which had been nothing short of a disaster. George had tried her best not to keep comparing Bear to Timmy, but it was hard not to when Bear kept refusing the jumps. To make matters worse, when she'd been trying simple circles and serpentines for the dressage, she slipped off Bear right in front of Misty and Dream, despite working really hard to adjust her riding for Bear.

The whole practice session had been terrible, and the pressure was on. Like Misty, everyone was keen to prove they were good enough to be on the school team and other girls in different houses were booking the thirty-minute slots in the arena. Every practice mattered.

Misty and Dream, however, had performed an incredible dressage-to-music routine. It looked like they were dancing together – every movement had been so graceful and beautiful. Katie and Sheriff had been amazing too, soaring over the jumps with ease. They'd only knocked one pole off the triple, which was pretty awesome. As for Lili and Ted? They'd been brilliant. George had loved watching them. Every jump had been perfect, every stride faultless.

Although George was genuinely happy about how well her friends had done, watching them made her feel worse about herself. She'd seen other girls from Stroller House practising too, girls who hadn't been able to bring their own horses because she'd won a riding place. George felt like everything she did was somehow letting them all down.

"Some star rider I turned out to be," George muttered now, scuffing her boot in the dirt as she made her way to the field to get Bear. Right now, George didn't even feel like she deserved her place at Paddock Grove. The others had offered to help her practise more, but she felt humiliated that she needed so much extra help.

Walking towards Bear and Ophelia's field, she could see Ophelia happily grazing away, but Bear was nowhere to be seen.

"Bear?" George clambered over the fence, checking to see if he was behind the trees on the far side. "Bear, where are you? *Bear*."

Panicked, George's eyes darted along the fence line, searching for any sign of Bear's usual escape tricks. But the paddock fence looked intact – no broken rails, no trampled grass, nothing to say that Bear had forced his way out. So where was he?

Not having her phone on her, George began to race back, hopping over a fence to cut through the fields to where she knew Katie was lunging Sheriff. But as she rounded the corner by the bottom of the cross-country course, she spotted a small paddock she'd never noticed before. There, cantering up and down the fence line with his ears pinned back, eyes wide, looking distressed, was Bear.

George rushed to the gate, grabbing the lead rope, which had been thrown on the ground.

"Bear, what are you doing in here?" She sprinted into the field, wanting to stop Bear cantering around, then she slowed down, not wanting to spook him any further. Surely the field management team wouldn't have taken him away from Ophelia?

"Bear? It's alright, Bear... Shhh, that's it, steady... Steady, Bear." George spoke softly as she walked towards him. For a moment, she thought he was going to continue to charge around, but he looked at her and whinnied, slowing into a trot before making his way over to her.

"Who put you in here, hey?" She stroked Bear, noticing how sweaty he was. "Well, whoever it was shouldn't have done." Then she clipped the lead rope to Bear's field head collar. "Come on, let's get you back to the stable." George patted him on his neck. "How about I get you a bag of haylage?"

He nudged her with his head and George grinned. Then he nudged her again a little harder. "Oh Bear, what am I going to do with you?" George giggled.

He put his head in the air and curled his lip as if he was trying to tell her something.

"I'm sorry, Bear. I'm so sorry. I'm sorry for how I've been treating you. I just... I just... I just miss Timmy." A pang of guilt shot through her. Bear was right in front of her, yet she was still hankering for Timmy.

As they walked back to the yard, George wondered why Bear had been moved. Mr Thatcher hadn't said anything to her when she'd seen him earlier. It upset her that no one had told her. She hated the idea of Bear being so stressed and lonely.

George put Bear back in his stable and was about to get a handful of treats from the feed room when she saw Miss Fox, the vet, wander through the yard to see Dream, who had seemed slightly lame this morning when Misty had turned her out. George liked Miss Fox a lot. She really cared about the horses and on the first day when she'd given Bear a check-over, she'd been nothing but kind to both her and Bear.

"Miss Fox!" George called.

Miss Fox smiled before her expression turned to worry. "George, are you alright? What's wrong? Is there anything I can do?" Miss Fox was dressed in a brown leather jacket and jodhpurs, and her auburn hair was tied back into a long plait.

"I'm a bit worried about Bear."

"Why, what's happened?"

"I found him in the back paddock on his own. I'm not sure why he was in there, but he was running around really upset."

Miss Fox ran her hand along his legs. "Is he lame at all?"

George shook her head. "No, I don't think so – he just seemed frightened."

"OK, well why don't you put him in his stable and I'll come and check him later to make sure he hasn't pulled anything?"

"Thank you." George was grateful.

Miss Fox wandered off, and George went to see Katie and Lili. She explained what had happened and apologized for not going to the inter-house teatime practice session they'd arranged. She just didn't feel up to it, and Bear certainly didn't look up to it either.

There were lots of girls milling about tending their horses by the time George returned to the hay barn to prepare a large haylage bag for Bear, which he tucked into straight away. Then she grabbed her grooming kit from the wash-down area and set about grooming him in the stable.

George calmly and carefully worked the body brush over Bear's damp coat, feeling his solid muscles underneath each of her gentle strokes. Steam rose from his back in the cool air, the sweat making his coat dark and patchy.

"Is that better, Bear?" She spoke to him soothingly and Bear turned his head, lips twitching hopefully at her pocket for the treat she had in there for him.

"When I've finished, I'll give it to you." She moved to his face with the soft brush, then used her fingers to carefully scratch off the bit of dried mud near his forelock. By halfway through, Bear seemed much calmer.

Grabbing the mane comb out of her box, George spotted Meg and Jessica. "I'll be back in a minute, Bear." She patted him and made her way out of the stable.

"Meg!" George hurried towards her. "Why was Bear in the back paddock on his own?"

Meg's lips curled into a smirk. "Why do you think? Duh, I already told you, I don't want that scruffy pony with Ophelia. He's a bad influence, and if Mr Thatcher and Mrs Hawksworth won't do anything about it, I will." Her Californian lilt gave emphasis to her words.

"But you can't do that. You *can't* just put Bear in a paddock on his own. He isn't your horse – you can't just decide to move him."

She smirked again. "Whoops ... looks like I just did."

"Bear is mine, Meg."

"Well, you care about your little pony, and I'll care about my horse. Ophelia is better off without him and that's all that matters to me."

George was so upset. "He doesn't like being on his own! You know most horses don't like to be left on their own."

Jessica grinned as Meg shrugged. "Well, Ophelia isn't *most* horses. She was fine, and that's all I care about." They turned to go, but Meg stopped. "Oh, I hope you're not going to snitch to Mrs Hawksworth. No one likes a rat."

Chapter Fifteen

GEORGE'S NIGHTMARE

Later that evening, George stood outside Bear's stable, her frustration mounting with each passing minute.

"Bear, come on, what's the matter with you?" she sighed, as she tried to pull Bear with the lead rope attached to his head collar.

She'd put her name down every day to get a slot in the indoor school, and finally she'd got one, but now Bear wasn't moving. She'd been planning to take him to practise basic changes – walk to trot, trot to walk, walk to canter – just so she could get a better a sense of him. *Dance with him,* as Lili had said. George smiled at that thought, but it didn't stop the ever-growing annoyance as Bear planted his hooves firmly. How was she supposed to learn any new steps with a dance partner who wouldn't budge?

Bear continued to refuse to move, despite her coaxing and bribing him with a Polo mint. (That he'd turned down, which was unlike Bear.)

A group of giggling Year Nine girls walked past, eyeing her struggle, and George's cheeks burnt hot. She quickly turned back, determined to get Bear moving.

"You're embarrassing me," she said crossly. "Come on, Bear, you can't just stand there." Yet again, George pulled on Bear's lead rope. He took a single step forward, then immediately stopped.

George felt tears of frustration prickling at the corners of her eyes. "Fine, then, if that's the way you're going to be, why should I bother?" She undid his head collar. "Everyone says that I need to have more patience with you, but maybe it's you that needs to stop being so difficult."

Like earlier, Bear nudged her – unlike earlier, George didn't laugh.

"No, Bear, I'm not playing."

"Having trouble?"

George turned to see Katie approaching, dressed in her riding gear.

"Bear won't come out," George mumbled. "He's being so difficult."

Katie frowned, peering into the stable. "That's odd. He's usually keen to come out, isn't he? Has he been eating and drinking normally?"

"I think so. I brought him in from the paddock earlier and he seemed alright."

Katie glanced at Bear's haylage bag. "He hasn't eaten any of his haylage. Are you sure he's alright?"

"He's just being stubborn. You know how he is. Miss Fox came to see him, so he's been checked over."

Katie's frown deepened. "Maybe there's something wrong with him since then. Have you checked his temperature or pressed his tummy?"

"He's fine," George sighed. Katie had mentioned that her parents were vets, so she was probably trying to help, but George felt guilty for making a fuss.

Katie didn't look so certain. "Maybe we should get Miss Fox to have a look at him again?"

George shook her head. "I don't want to bother her just because Bear is being silly." *And I'm over-reacting.*

"Well if you're sure, but keep an eye on him… I better

go. My saddle keeps slipping so Ms Stopcroft said she'll have a look in case I need to see the saddler next week."

Bear nudged George again, but she shook her head. "I already told you, I'm not playing. Why do you have to be so difficult?" She really thought they had been getting somewhere, but after another fifteen minutes, George gave up. She checked the locks of the stable door and marched away, swiping away tears of frustration and leaving Bear on his own.

Later that night, there was a loud knock on the dormitory door that jolted George and the others awake. George sat up in bed, not knowing what the time was – although she could see it was still pitch-black outside.

It was Mrs Winters, the housemistress who stayed in Stroller House overnight, her worried face illuminated by the beam of her torch.

"George – it's Bear." Mrs Winters spoke quietly but urgently. "He's not very well. You need to come straight away."

The words hit George like a bucket of ice water. "Why, what's happened?"

She scrambled out of bed as she spoke, grabbing a jumper and putting it on over her pyjamas. She slipped on some thick socks and her boots and hurried to follow Mrs Winters.

"Shall someone go with her?" Lili's voice came from out of the darkness. "If that's what George wants?"

Mrs Winters hesitated, then nodded. "George, would you like that?"

"Yes please." She could hardly speak.

"Alright, just one of you, though… Katie, why don't you go with her? Quickly now, both of you."

Katie and George hurried after Mrs Winters, Katie reaching for George's hand and giving it a squeeze as the three of them made their way down the path towards the stables. There was a light on in Bear's stable block and they hurried inside to where Mr Thatcher was standing by Bear's stall.

George gasped. Bear was lying down on the soft wood shavings with Miss Fox kneeling over him.

"Bear, oh my gosh, *Bear*."

Miss Fox turned and gave her a small smile, but George could see how worried she looked.

"I'm glad you're here, George, and I'm sure Bear is too." She stroked his face, and George could see that Bear was struggling to breathe properly. His coat was damp and he was trembling.

"What's happened to him?" George knelt by Bear's head and gently placed her hand on his face.

"Mr Thatcher and I think it's probably sycamore poisoning, I'm afraid."

"Miss Fox said you'd caught him in the small paddock by the cross-country course?" Mr Thatcher asked.

George nodded. "Meg put him there." She wiped away her tears, not caring about being a rat when all she could think about was how sick Bear was.

"She probably didn't realize," Mr Thatcher said, his face tight with worry. "The sycamore's hidden behind the other trees, but that's why we don't use that field for horses. Bear probably ate some of the sycamore seeds."

The adults started talking about cutting the tree down, but that wouldn't change what was happening to Bear now.

George looked at Bear. She stroked his ears, shuffling herself nearer. "Is it serious, Miss Fox?"

Miss Fox glanced quickly at Mr Thatcher, then back to George. "I'm afraid so. We caught it early, which is good. But I can't make any promises. I'm so sorry."

Katie rushed up and hugged George.

"Shouldn't we take him to an equine hospital?" she asked as George stroked Bear's face.

Miss Fox shook her head. "The nearest one is too far away, and Bear is too poorly to travel right now." She gave a sad smile. "They wouldn't be able to do any more than we are, but Bear seems to be a fighter. Let's hope he pulls through."

"Can I stay with him?" George asked.

Miss Fox nodded. "Of course. Katie, why don't you go back to the dorm? I'll walk you over."

While Mr Thatcher went to fetch her a coat to keep warm, George continued to stroke Bear's face. She leant in, whispering in his ear. "Come on, Bear, *please* get better … please. I know I haven't been much of a friend to you, but I'll try harder, I really will. Bear, please pull through."

The stable was quiet except for the soft sounds of horses moving, and throughout the night George watched anxiously as Miss Fox and Mr Thatcher worked hard to make Bear as comfortable as possible and nurse him back to health while she spoke to him gently. She didn't want to think about Bear not pulling through, and she didn't even care if he wasn't able to jump over a fence or do a figure of eight, or even bother to lunge. All she wanted was for him to get better.

She moved her hand softly over his coat, her tears dropping into it as she imagined all the mischief he might get up to if he pulled through. With each passing moment, George realized how much she loved him.

As the sky began to lighten, Bear's breathing began to get slower and more normal. Then he suddenly lifted his head a bit and made a quiet whinny as he looked at George.

"Did you see that? Did you see that, Miss Fox?"

Miss Fox nodded from where she was leaning over the stable door, her hands wrapped around a mug of steaming hot tea that Mr Thatcher had brewed. "I did, George. He looks like he's improving. We're not out of the woods yet, but this is a good sign." She looked at Mr Thatcher, who spoke up in his gruff voice.

"He's a fighter alright, and you being here with him probably helped a lot."

Relief flooded through George and she hugged Bear's neck. "We're a team, you and me, I promise."

"Maybe we could see if we can stand him up?" Miss Fox said. "It's better for him to try to move around."

"Come on, Bear. Let's see if we can get you up."

"Stand back." Mr Thatcher directed George to move towards the stable door so Bear would have enough space to stand, then encouraged him to get up, using his hands to guide and support him. "Come on, boy, let's see what you're like on your feet."

George held her breath as she watched, and with only a moment's hesitation, Bear pushed himself up and stood on wobbly legs facing her. She stroked his soft nose.

"I think the worst is definitely over now," Miss Fox breathed, relief in her voice.

"Did you hear that, Bear? You're going to be alright." She kissed his nose.

"Miss Harris." From behind, George heard Mrs Hawksworth. She turned to see her striding towards them, impeccably dressed despite how early it was.

Mrs Hawksworth's eyes quickly scanned the scene, genuine relief in the headmistress's eyes as she looked at Bear. "I see our patient is on the mend," she said, her voice softer than usual. She approached Bear, gently patting his neck. "Well done Miss Fox, Mr Thatcher... And well done to you, Miss Harris, for staying with him. I'm sure that made a huge difference too. He'll have known that he was in the best of hands with people who loved him."

George nodded, surprised by the praise. But Mrs Hawksworth's expression suddenly changed as she looked towards the stable block entrance.

Standing there was the last person George expected to see: Meg.

"Miss Lopez?" Mrs Hawksworth squared her shoulders.

Meg shuffled forward, her eyes downcast.

"What are you doing in the stables at this time? You know the yard's off-limits until seven a.m. for girls."

"I … I heard about Bear. I was worried. I wanted to know if he was alright."

"A little late for that, don't you think, Miss Lopez? I have heard from Mr Thatcher what happened regarding your decision to move Bear to the small paddock – a decision that was not yours to make."

Meg's head shot up to look at Mrs Hawksworth. "I didn't know that Bear would become ill. I wouldn't have done it if—"

"While I understand and believe you didn't intend to cause harm to Bear," Mrs Hawksworth said, her tone leaving no room for argument, "it is not your place to rearrange the horses, do you understand? That decision lies with Mr Thatcher *for a reason*," she said firmly. "At Paddock Grove, we value discipline and care because to do otherwise is to cause harm. Actions, as you can see, have consequences. Serious ones."

Meg was red-faced and, despite everything that had happened, George felt a twinge of sympathy. She wouldn't like to be on the receiving end of their headmistress's wrath.

Meg looked like she was going to say something,

but Mrs Hawksworth held up a hand, silencing her. "Thankfully, due to Miss Fox and Mr Thatcher's quick thinking, Bear has made a wonderful recovery. But I cannot let this behaviour go unchecked. As it stands, you will not be able to try out for the school team this term."

"But Mrs Hawksworth…" Meg started to protest. "That's not fair, that's—"

"Exactly what comes from your own actions," Mrs Hawksworth cut her off firmly. "My decision is not open for discussion, Miss Lopez. You'll also be reporting to Mr Thatcher for stable duties for the next month. Perhaps that will help you appreciate the responsibility we hold towards these animals."

Meg was wide-eyed. "But … but… I can't— I *don't* muck out, Mrs Hawksworth!"

"Unless you want me to make it two months, I suggest you face your mistake head-on and learn from this."

When Meg turned away to hurry from the yard, Mrs Hawksworth's expression softened as she looked back at Bear and George.

“I’m glad to see he’s improving, Miss Harris. Never forget, it’s a true honour to have horses and ponies in our lives. Cherish and respect that gift always.” With that, Mrs Hawksworth strode out of the yard after Meg.

George turned back to Bear and rested her head on his. “You and me, Bear, for ever.”

As the sun rose higher over Paddock Grove, George knew that things were going to be different now. Bear wasn’t just any old pony. He was her friend, and she promised herself she’d never forget how special he truly was. George had been so focused on wanting a horse that could win a competition that she’d not realized Bear had won her heart. Now that he had pulled through – now that she knew she loved him – George promised herself that from this moment on she and Bear were a team.

Chapter Sixteen

AN EXCITING ANNOUNCEMENT

Just over a week later, George stood in Bear's stable, running her hand over his neck. He certainly seemed to be back to his old self, his eyes alert and playful. She'd been grooming him daily and Mr Thatcher had got one of the yard staff to give him a blanket clip, so he was looking very smart. He'd also managed to break out of his stable again and had been found by Mrs Winters eating grass near Ted's paddock, which George thought meant he must be feeling better.

Katie had been brilliant, and helped look after Bear with her. She knew a lot about caring for ponies, and George guessed that was because both Katie's parents were equine vets. Katie's confidence with Bear had rubbed off on George, and she hoped that it would be a new start for her and Bear. She'd also been riding some of the school's horses while Bear was resting up, and it occurred to George that she'd been so used to riding Timmy that she'd fallen into bad habits.

Bear nudged George, breaking her thoughts to see if there were any treats in her pocket. "Hey, Bear, I've nothing in there apart from a hoof pick," George laughed, gently pushing his nose away.

Lili leant on the stable door, grinning. "It's good to see him so happy again. Mr Thatcher said that now he's able to be turned out again, he can share Ted's paddock."

George was delighted. "That's brilliant news." She'd been worried that he'd have to share with Ophelia again. Not that she minded Bear being with Ophelia – it was Meg she didn't want to be near.

Since Meg had been told she wasn't allowed to try out for the team, she and her friends had been giving George dirty looks. Meg hadn't apologized either, although George had heard her tell Mrs Hawksworth that she had when she'd been questioned about it. George didn't care; all she cared about was Bear.

"Anyway, I've got this for you," Lili added before reaching into her pocket and pulling out a small, round device. "Well, it's for Bear really. It's an AirTag. I had one spare, and I thought you could attach it to his field collar. That way, if he does wander off, or break down the fence again, we can find him quickly by tracking him on our phones." She smiled brightly as she held it out. "Consider it a gift."

George couldn't believe how kind Lili was being. "Lili, this is amazing. Are you sure? I know they're not cheap."

Lili shrugged. "Don't worry about that – anyway, it'll save us all a lot of headaches if he does escape."

George laughed and looked at Bear, who was playing with the latch on his stable door with his teeth. "You hear that, Bear? You won't be able to play hide-and-seek now."

As they attached the AirTag to Bear's field collar, George wondered how she'd ever been disappointed in him.

"Thanks, Lili," she murmured. "For everything."

Lili smiled. "That's what friends are for."

George smiled back at her. "Do you want to go to the library to do the French homework Mr Linson gave us?"

A twinkle came into Lili's eyes. "Nope. I'm going to get Misty to do it for me."

"Misty?"

"Yup. Why not? Misty's French, and I have a French assignment – seems to me the perfect plan." She skipped around the aisle between the stalls like she hadn't a care in the world. "No assignment means more riding for me."

"Aren't you worried about getting into trouble?" George asked.

Lili pulled a face. "You sound like Katie now."

Just then, Mrs Hawksworth appeared. "Miss Harris?"

"Good afternoon, Mrs Hawksworth," George said, suddenly nervous as a group of much older girls walked past, looking over curiously.

"I'm glad I caught you." Mrs Hawksworth came to a stop by Bear's stable, with Lili hovering a little way away, clearly listening in as she petted one of the nearby horses. "I have some news I think you'll find exciting."

George's heart skipped. She had no idea what that news could be.

"Representatives from Whistlejacket, the sponsors of your scholarship, are planning to visit next week. They want to see you and Bear in action – they're also planning to bring a photographer and a journalist with them." Mrs Hawksworth gave a wide smile. "Plus they want to do an interview with you, as this year's scholarship recipient, and take photos of you and Bear for their marketing campaign to feature in *Riding Joy Monthly*."

Excitement bubbled up in George's chest. "That's … that's amazing." She only just managed to get the words out. She had posters on her wall and articles from the magazine she'd saved at home, and now she was going to feature in it!

"Since Whistlejacket is a luxury equine clothing brand, they have been kind enough to craft a bespoke outfit for you featuring their signature jodhpurs, riding jacket and hat. All adorned with the Paddock Grove logo, of course. They're also providing a brand-new saddle and bridle for Bear, which is wonderful news. A professional saddle fitter will visit this week to ensure a perfect fit."

Mrs. Hawksworth's words were clipped but warm.

George glanced at Lili and couldn't hide her smile.

"I've discussed this generous offer with your parents, and they've given their full permission for it to go ahead. Whistlejacket are gifting you these items as part of their sponsorship. You should be thrilled, Miss Harris. You're one very lucky girl."

George was barely listening as she exchanged more excited glances with Lili over Mrs Hawksworth's shoulder.

"Do you know what day they'll be coming?" George was breathless.

"Next Friday. Miss Fox assures me that Bear is perfectly fit now for you to start riding him from today to get him well-schooled by then. We shall host a special luncheon for our guests, as they've been generous sponsors of the scholarship programme for several years now. Weather permitting, we hope to hold the luncheon outdoors, then afterwards you'll have your photoshoot." Mrs Hawksworth glanced over the stable door at Bear, a faint look of concern flashing across her face, there and then gone. "No doubt you'll want to make the best impression possible. This is an excellent opportunity for you to showcase your skills and represent Paddock Grove, so I trust you'll have Bear groomed to perfection?"

George nodded. "Yes, Mrs Hawksworth. We'll be ready."

"And I'll help!" Lili blurted out. She sounded as thrilled as George felt, clearly forgetting that Mrs Hawksworth hadn't actually been talking to her.

"Good." Mrs Hawksworth gave them both a proud look. "In togetherness we ride to the stars in strength."

And as she always did, Mrs Hawksworth strode away abruptly, leaving George almost unable to contain her excitement. She turned back to Bear. "Did you hear that? We're going to do a photoshoot and the whole world will be able to see how amazing you are." She hugged him, then hugged Lili, bouncing around the stable block in excitement.

"What are you two looking so pleased about?" Meg's voice cut through the air from behind them.

George turned to see Meg and Jessica staring at them. "Nothing."

"It can't be *nothing*," Meg commented, chin tipped

up so she could look down her nose at them.

"If you must know," Lili said proudly, "George is going to be in a magazine. The sponsors of her scholarship are coming to interview her and take photos of her and Bear."

George appreciated her friend's delight, but wished Lili hadn't told Meg and Jessica – they were the last people she wanted to know.

"Who would want to read about *them*?" Meg sneered.

Jessica's nasty laugh bounced off the rafters. "I wouldn't." And with that, the two of them wandered away.

"Why did you tell them, Lili?" George said, trying not to be cross.

Lili shrugged. "Because they're always thinking they're better than anyone else. Anyway, I didn't know it was supposed to be a secret."

"It's fine," George sighed. "All that matters is Bear looking amazing on the day."

Chapter Seventeen

THE BIG DAY ARRIVES

The following week passed in a whirlwind of preparation and joy for George. Lili and Katie rallied round her, and even Tabitha joined in a bit. Since Tabitha had told her about her horse, Petra, George understood why she was often upset that she had to ride the school's horses and felt left out.

Misty helped put George through her dressage paces in case the representatives from Whistlejacket wanted to see her perform more than one discipline. Both Katie and Tabitha (who was particularly interested in course building) helped George plan some rigorous grid work to help Bear improve his jumping and gave George plenty of practice in how best to ride him over increasingly tricky combinations. Best of all, the saddle fitter brought not only a general and a jump saddle but also a deep-seated dressage saddle that felt to George like she was sitting in the comfiest armchair. Three saddles, all for Bear!

Late Thursday night, George, Lili and Katie had spent hours washing and grooming Bear until his coat shone and his hooves gleamed with oil. They'd all been covered in dirt by the time they'd finished, but it had been worth it to see Bear looking so stunning. Now Friday morning was here, George suddenly felt incredibly nervous. She was dressed in white jodhpurs, blue patent leather riding boots, a matching riding jacket and a white polo top. She'd never felt as smart in her life. She only wished that her parents were here to see her.

"How are you feeling? Are you nervous?" Lili asked. "You look amazing in your outfit."

George nodded as they stood outside Bear's stable. "Look, my hands are even shaking." But she beamed with pride. "I think all our hard work has paid off, don't you?"

Katie laughed. "Totally! And I know you're going to be incredible today, and you look amazing too… Come on, let's go! Mrs Winters said they'll be serving lunch on the lawn in fifteen minutes, but they want us there beforehand."

"I'm so pleased Mrs Hawksworth let you and Katie and Misty be part of the day. It makes it even more special," George said as she followed Lili. The sun was out, and the chefs had made a beautiful buffet lunch, which they'd laid out on the tables under the cherry trees. Everything was perfect.

"Girls, hurry, Mrs Hawksworth is already on the lawn with our guests." Mr Bassey, the bursar, cut an imposing figure. He had flawless ebony skin and a trimmed beard and today he was wearing a crisp white shirt and blue suit. Lili had told George that, like a lot of the Paddock Grove staff, Mr Bassey was an incredible rider, and George wondered whether she would ever see him on a horse as they followed him.

When they rounded the corner, George paused for a moment, taking in all the people milling on the neatly trimmed lawn. They had all come to see her.

"You'll be great," Lili said, as Katie reached out and gave George's arm an encouraging squeeze. "You're going to show them how fantastic you and Bear are."

George walked towards Mrs Hawksworth, who was speaking to a group of men and women. "Ah, Miss Harris, these are the people from Whistlejacket – they're very keen to talk to you."

George nodded and smiled, but by the time the lunch was over, her nerves were at fever pitch. She'd barely been able to eat anything, although the pasta salad, vegetarian Thai green curry and chicken chasseur, along with the slow-cooked lamb and roast potatoes, looked and smelt delicious.

"Are you ready, Miss Harris?" Mrs Hawksworth asked. "Maybe you can bring Bear over, then we'll go to the main arena. After you've ridden, then you can go and do your interview. And Miss Harris? Remember, it's your talent rather than luck that's got you here. Enjoy your moment." She nodded and wandered back to the guests.

George hurried to the yard with Mrs Hawksworth's encouraging words in her head, but just as she was getting near to the tack room to get Bear's saddle and bridle, she heard a noise followed by giggling.

She frowned when she saw Meg and her friends coming from the direction of the stables.

Meg gave her a haughty look, a smirk playing on her lips. "Oh, hi, George, how's the lunch going?"

George was puzzled. Meg was never nice to her. "It's going fine, thanks," she muttered, then walked into the tack room to grab her things.

"We just thought we'd come and admire your pony, didn't we, Jess?" Meg stood in the doorway watching her.

Jessica nodded, then smiled at Harriet. They both had smug expressions on their faces.

"Enjoy the rest of the day; it should be fun," Meg called, before she wandered away with the others.

George was pleased they'd gone. She rushed to pick up her girth and the gold-coloured numnah the company had given her – she didn't want to make people wait – and hurried out to tack up Bear.

The moment George stepped into the yard, she heard the distinct clatter of hooves. Her heart dropped. There was Bear trotting across the cobblestones.

"Oh no … no … *Bear*, no," she called out, dropping her tack on the floor to go after him. How did he get out? Mr Thatcher had put a double lock on his door yesterday! *"Bear."*

"Whoops, looks like your donkey is on the loose." Meg was leaning on the wall by the feed room. "That'll teach you for getting me kicked off the team." She narrowed her eyes meanly. "You better run, if you want to get him back!"

"I can't believe you let him out!" Upset as she was, George didn't have time to say anything else. She needed to catch Bear before he reached the lunch.

Launching into a sprint after him, George ran as fast as she could, calling Bear's name.

And that's when it happened.

As she turned the corner, a paper napkin fluttered towards them, and Bear – usually so stoical and unflustered – spooked at the sight of it, his eyes wide as he snorted … and he bolted straight across the lawn towards the buffet.

"Bear!" But it was too late. Bear cantered towards the crowd, knocking a table onto the floor. A lady from Whistlejacket toppled off her chair, and the man George had been talking to earlier, who was head of marketing, tripped backwards into one of the rose bushes.

People screamed and jumped out of the way as Bear continued to rampage. Plates crashed to the ground, glasses shattered and the fancy canapés went flying.

George continued to race after Bear, but he ignored her, cantering on, heading straight for the shallow pond by the old oak tree. He thundered past a startled Mrs Hawksworth and splashed into the water.

"Oh no, Bear!" George groaned loudly as Bear dropped and rolled, coating himself in thick mud. As she reached the pond's edge, her foot slipped on the wet grass. With a yelp, George tumbled forward too; she tried to stop herself falling, but she found herself landing right next to Bear in the water.

"Miss Harris!" Mrs Hawksworth's shocked voice cut through the air. *"Miss Harris!"*

George squeezed her eyes shut, wishing – as she had on the first day – that she could vanish into thin air. Although this time she wasn't cross with Bear. This time her anger was directed firmly where it belonged: at Meg.

With mud dripping from her hair, she peeked her eyes open. There stood Mrs Hawksworth, and behind her, the representatives of Whistlejacket, all staring with wide eyes and open mouths.

Bear, oblivious to the chaos he'd just caused, stood up and happily shook himself, splattering everyone with mud.

A tall man with a very bushy moustache stepped forward to glare at George and Bear.

"This is totally unacceptable." He turned to Mrs Hawksworth. "We can't possibly photograph them like this."

"I'm really sorry," George mumbled. "If you give me a bit of time, I can clean—"

"There is no time." The man's mouth was set in a firm line. "We're on a tight schedule." His bulging eyes scanned the crowd of students. "We need another pair…"

Chapter Eighteen

THE WORST NEWS

George was finishing mucking out Bear's stable. She was trying not to feel too down about the afternoon's escapades, so she was keeping herself busy. Bear nudged her shoulder gently and she smiled.

"There you go, all clean for the night." She wrapped her arms around his neck. "Oh Bear," she said, her voice wobbling. "That wasn't how it was supposed to go."

Bear whinnied softly in response, as if agreeing with her, and George squeezed him tightly.

About to leave, George heard footsteps approaching. Turning, she saw Lili walking towards her.

"George?" Lili called out hesitantly. "Can we talk?"

George nodded. She could see that Lili looked upset. "Sure. Is everything alright?"

Lili twisted her top nervously. "I … I wanted to say sorry. About the photos and the interview."

After Bear had crashed the lunch, the Whistlejacket people had insisted on finding someone else to model their clothes and had chosen the most beautiful horse in the yard: Ted. Lili was still wearing the Whistlejacket-branded clothing. (George's were in the laundry – she wasn't sure the stains would ever come out…)

She didn't hold any anger towards Lili – at least it wasn't Meg! All George felt was disappointment for her and Bear. It would've been amazing to have been in the magazine. She would've been so proud to be featured with Bear.

"I feel terrible for taking your place," Lili said, her voice quiet. "It should have been you and Bear, not me and Ted."

George squeezed her hand and battled not to show how disappointed she already did. She didn't want Lili to feel any worse than she was. "It's not your fault, Lili, and besides … Ted looked amazing. So did you."

Lili shook her head. "But it's not fair. You're the one on the scholarship, so you should be the one who gets the recognition." She paused for a moment. "You're not cross with me?"

"No, of course not! Never. It's Meg I'm angry at... She's the one who let Bear out of his stable."

"What?" Lili's eyes widened.

Before George could say anything else, they saw Mrs Winters, the housemistress, heading towards them. She looked very serious.

"George, Mrs Hawksworth would like to see you in her office with Mr Bassey," she said gently.

George's stomach tightened. She was in no doubt that Mrs Hawksworth was going to discipline her.

Mrs Winters glanced at Lili. "If I told you to stay here, Lili, I don't suppose it would have any effect. Come on, you can wait for George outside the office."

George quickly checked both the stable locks, then she and Lili followed Mrs Winters through the yard and into the school, hurrying along the long corridors and up the back staircases to Mrs Hawksworth's office.

Mrs Winters bid Lili wait in a wooden chair outside the office, then she knocked on the large oak doors.

"Come in."

Mrs Winters smiled at George as they entered the imposing room. This was the first time she'd been in the headmistress's office. It was massive, with an enormous carved wooden desk by the window. The walls were covered in glass shelves with trophies and school photos, as well as photographs of someone George assumed was a young Mrs Hawksworth competing in various riding competitions.

"Hello, Miss Harris." Mrs Hawksworth looked up from her desk. "Please, come and sit down."

"Hello, Miss Harris." Mr Bassey stood by Mrs Hawksworth's desk, echoing the headmistress's welcome.

George could feel herself shaking. She had no idea what this was about, but it looked serious.

Mrs Winters continued to stand while George went to perch on the edge of the hard leather chair in front of the desk.

"I'm afraid I have some rather difficult news," Mrs Hawksworth began. "As you can imagine, the Whistlejacket representatives were less than impressed with today's events." She paused, her eyes full of sympathy. "I'm so sorry, but they've informed us that they wish to cancel your scholarship at the end of the autumn term."

The words hit George like a punch in the chest. Her shoulders slumped. This couldn't be happening. Just as she'd started to feel like she belonged at Paddock Grove, it was about to be snatched away. She'd made wonderful friends, she and Bear had become a team, but now she was going to lose it all because of one muddy incident... All because of *Meg.*

"Can they do that?" she whispered. "Can they really cancel the scholarship? After only one term?"

Mr Bassey nodded. "I'm afraid they can."

George glanced at the bursar. "Can't you get them to change their minds?"

"I've tried to persuade the sponsors to reconsider," Mrs Hawksworth said. "But unfortunately they feel, after what happened today, that you and Bear don't fit the image of their brand." She paused, her eyes full of sympathy. "What they're doing is cruel, but it comes down to money, and they don't want to invest in a horse and rider who don't fit their brand. I'm so sorry."

Through her tears, George felt her dream vanishing right in front of her. The half term holiday was barely two weeks away. After that she and Bear would only be able to stay until Christmas. There was no way her parents could afford to send her here, not even for one term.

"Is there really nothing we can do?" George asked quietly.

Mrs Hawksworth shook her head. "I'm afraid not. As I say, the decision has been made. But you still have the rest of this term. We'll do everything we can to help support you, and of course I've already spoken to your parents, but I'm sure you'd like to call them too. If you need anything, anything at all, my door is always open. Remember, Miss Harris, this doesn't change how talented you are."

"I'm truly sorry, Miss Harris," Mr Bassey added.

Mrs Hawksworth glanced at Mrs Winters, who'd been standing silently. "Perhaps you'd like to take Miss Harris back to the dormitories now."

"Certainly." Mrs Winters led George out of the office.

George saw Lili and immediately burst into tears. Without words, Lili hugged her tightly.

"What happened?" she asked eventually. "What did Mrs Hawksworth say?"

George tried to explain through her tears, but then the worst thought of all occurred to her. That if she couldn't stay at Paddock Grove, then her parents would not be able to afford for her keep Bear at all. Her scholarship covered nearly all the cost of his upkeep.

Lili's eyes widened as she listened. "That's not fair, though!" Lili became upset too. "You didn't do anything wrong. George, I'm so sorry."

"What am I going to do, Lili? I don't want to leave. I love it here and so does Bear." She sighed miserably. Her future at the school had seemed so bright this morning and now her dream was over.

Chapter Nineteen

A PUZZLE

It was chilly and drizzly as George raced across the yard clutching a glossy magazine in her hands. Colourful leaves crunched under her feet as she followed the track up to one of the paddocks.

Despite the awful week she'd had ever since Mrs Hawksworth had told her the news about having to leave, today she was excited. The magazine had arrived, and even though she wasn't in it, she couldn't wait to show Lili the photos.

"Lili! Lili!" George called. She waved at Lili, who was checking for rabbit holes where Ted and Bear were grazing. An older girl's horse had stumbled into a rabbit hole when he'd been charging around in his paddock, and Mr Thatcher had told all the students to check for them.

Panting, George slowed down at the gate. She smiled at Ted and Bear, who'd become inseparable. Ted didn't even like leaving the field before Bear, and they had to bring them in at the same time now.

Lili's face broke into a smile as she saw George. "I haven't found one hole, which is good, although I did find Ted's fly mask from last summer in the bushes!" she laughed.

George let herself into the paddock and skipped towards Lili. "It's here!"

"What is?"

"The magazine with your photos. They look amazing, Lili!"

Lili squealed. George quickly flipped through the glossy pages to get to the article about Lili.

"Here they are."

Lili gasped. The photographer had done a brilliant job. There was a photo of Lili and Ted mid-jump, with Ted looking beautiful and athletic, and Lili's posture perfect. There was another shot of her doing a superb flying change during her dressage routine, but the main photo was Lili on the ground stroking Ted.

"Oh, Lili." George stared at the photos. "You both look fantastic. Do you like them?"

Lili blushed.

"Thanks, George. It was fun doing the shoot. I'm only sorry you couldn't."

"You should send this to your parents," George said without thinking.

Lili didn't say anything and continued to read the article, but her face suddenly dropped. "Oh no."

"What is it?" George hadn't read it yet. She'd only glanced at the photos when Mrs Winters had handed her the magazine, then she'd run to find her friend.

Lili pointed to the small caption beneath one of the photos. "They've put how much Ted is worth. Who told them that? I never mentioned it during the interview." She sounded genuinely upset.

George looked, and tried to stop herself gasping as she read how much Ted was worth. It was more money than she had ever imagined. "Wow. I didn't realize he was…" George trailed off, not wanting to say anything more. How could Lili have such an expensive horse? But it didn't seem right to ask.

Wanting to change the subject, George turned the page. "Hey, that's the same story as Tabitha and I saw in the newspaper the other week about the horse thieves. I recognize the photos of the horse that was stolen from Willowbrook."

Lili leant over to look and began to read out loud. "*...The horse that was stolen from Willowbrook riding stables was just the latest in a recent spate of missing and stolen horses across the south coast of England...*" Lili looked up again. "What do you think they do with the horses?"

"Sell them on, I guess. Maybe they ship them abroad." Not wanting to think about it as it was too upsetting, George looked up and saw Meg in the distance bringing in Ophelia. George nodded towards Bear and Ted, who were grooming each other. "Look at those two!"

Lili laughed, but George thought she still looked a bit worried. "It's great how they've become such good friends."

"Bear's even happy not to try to escape as long as Ted's there with him." George sighed, thinking how little time she had left at Paddock Grove. She didn't want to spoil it by being sad, but it was very difficult not to be.

Just then, fat raindrops began to fall and the two girls hurried to catch their horses and bring them in. By the time they reached the yard, all of them – Lili and Ted and George and Bear – were wet through. After stripping them off and making sure Ted was dry enough to bed down, Lili came to watch George as she finished up with Bear.

Meg was waving a copy of the magazine. "Is your horse really worth that?" She crossed her arms and stood in front of them.

Lili gave her an angry look. "I've got nothing to say to you, Meg Lopez, not after what you did to Bear and George. It should be you leaving the school, not George."

Meg looked shocked for a moment, then said snootily, "I didn't do anything – and even if I *did* – how could I possibly have known it would mean George leaving?"

Lili frowned at her. "You never think anything bad you do will have consequences."

"It's not my fault George's parents can't afford to keep her here!"

"Why are you so horrible?"

"I'm only telling the truth. Unlike *some* people," Meg said, flicking her hair.

"What are you talking about?" Lili snapped.

Meg looked Lili up and down. "I'm talking about *you*, Lili. Do you know what I think? I think Ted isn't really your horse. If he was, your parents could afford for you to be on the full livery package, *not* DIY livery. I know you're lying about Ted. You must have loaned him from someone, but you're telling everyone he's yours. You're such a liar and I'm going to make sure everyone knows it."

Lili looked at Meg and shook her head, but she didn't say anything. Instead, she walked briskly away.

Meg stared at her as she left, then at George. "We're all thinking it, even you."

"Ted's Lili's. He doesn't belong to anyone but her."

Meg smirked. "Whatever."

She walked off, leaving George standing on her own. As much as she didn't have any time for Meg, she did wonder if what she'd said was true. But why would Lili lie about something like that?

Chapter Twenty

A CANTEEN CONFRONTATION

It was suppertime and the school canteen at Paddock Grove buzzed with chatter. Like so many parts of Paddock Grove, the canteen was large and airy. Windows lined both sides of the spacious hall, and the polished wooden floor gleamed.

George, Katie, Lili and Tabitha sat together at one of the long tables, each eating a steaming jacket potato piled high with melted cheese.

"Maybe if we all ask Mrs Hawksworth again, she'll change her mind," Lili said.

"She won't. There's nothing she can do," George said miserably as she took another bite of her potato.

"There must be something we can do," Katie said.

"There isn't, and I'm so worried that when I leave here my parents won't be able to afford to keep Bear." George was surprised to see Tabitha giving her a sympathetic smile.

"I'm sorry, George. I know what it's like to lose your best friend. I miss Petra every day."

"Won't your parents change their mind about getting you another horse?" Lili asked Tabitha.

"I don't want another horse. I want Petra," Tabitha snapped, looking very upset.

"Lili was only asking – she didn't mean anything by it," Katie said gently.

"Well, I don't want her to ask anything." Tabitha glared at Katie, then looked down and tucked into her potato.

There was a moment of awkward silence before Lili broke it. "So George, you know I hate Maths and you're really good at it..."

"Don't tell me you're going to ask her to do your assignment," Katie said seriously.

Lili shrugged. "No, I'm just asking her to help me." She grinned. "Not all of us are good at classwork."

"Maybe if you tried harder, Lili?" Katie replied.

Lili laughed. "That would mean there was less time to ride Ted."

George joined in then. "Maybe I should charge you for homework help and pay my fees that way?"

She needed to have a laugh with her friends – she didn't want to keep thinking about having to leave. She wanted to enjoy every moment she could, and she loved that Lili didn't worry much about anything. Even when she kept getting the lowest marks on her schoolwork, Lili didn't seem to care. (Although it did make George wonder what her parents thought when they got her school report at the end of each term.)

"Hey, Lili!" Meg called out from the table opposite, waving the magazine in the air. "We're all discussing your interview." She sat with Jessica and a group of other girls. "And we're trying to work out who Ted *actually* belongs to."

"Not this again," Katie muttered. She turned to Meg. "Why don't you just leave it?"

"Why should we when she's lying to everyone?"

Lili's smile faltered for a moment, but she sat up

straight, addressing Meg. "I'm not lying. I already told you, he's mine. He's been mine since he was a foal and I was a baby. My father bought him for me when I was born."

This was the first time George had heard about this.

Jessica's eyes narrowed. "But it says here what Ted's worth. There's no way you own a horse like that!"

"I don't care what you think. It's none of your business."

"No one believes you," Meg declared loudly, her voice carrying across the canteen. Several heads turned to watch the unfolding drama.

George looked at Lili, expecting to see her friend's usual confident grin. Instead, Lili's face had gone pale, her eyes fixed on her plate.

"Just ignore them," Katie said firmly, putting a hand on Lili's arm. "They're just jealous."

Tabitha frowned. "Is it true, though?" she asked, her voice low. "I mean, how can your parents afford a horse like that?"

"Tabitha!" Katie snapped.

"I just want to know, that's all," Tabitha snapped

back. "How could your dad afford Ted?"

Lili's shoulders visibly tensed. "I don't want to talk about it," she muttered, pushing a piece of potato around her plate.

"Oh, come on," Tabitha pushed. "We're your friends. You can tell us the truth."

"If you're her friend, why don't you just leave it?" Katie suggested.

"I'm allowed to ask," Tabitha replied.

"I *am* telling the truth," Lili insisted. "And it's nothing to do with you either."

"Well, I don't think you're telling the truth."

Lili pushed her chair back and stood up.

"Wait, Lili, don't go!" George urged her.

"I don't want to be around Tabitha."

"Then I'll come with you."

"I want to be on my own," Lili said, clearly battling tears. Then she turned and walked off, leaving her half-eaten potato behind. George watched her go – sorry for her, but unable to quite shake the feeling that there really *was* more to the story of Ted.

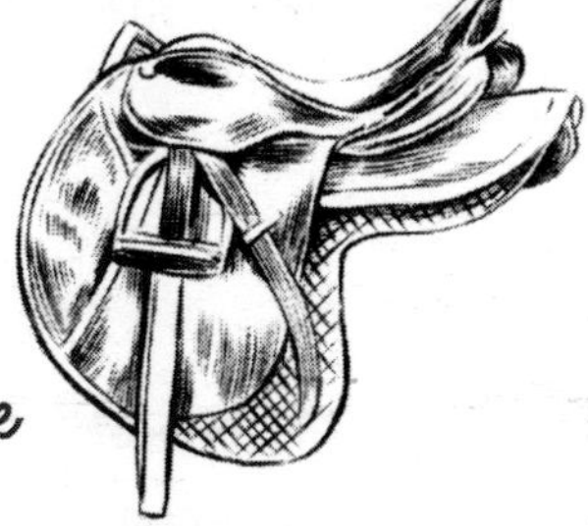

Chapter Twenty-One

A JUMPING CHANCE

It was early morning, and the hammering of rain on the roof of the indoor school echoed around as George sat on Bear. It hadn't stopped raining for the past couple of days, so most riding lessons had been inside – which George hadn't minded, although she knew that Bear preferred riding outside.

George loved the practice sessions that Ms Stopcroft ran before breakfast – even when she was only doing flatwork – but yesterday Ms Stopcroft had asked her to attend the advanced jumping session. George had been delighted that all her and Bear's hard work had paid off.

She had a lot to prove and wanted to show that Ms Stopcroft's faith in her was justified, and today the pressure was on. Her stomach was filled with butterflies, but it wasn't the horrid worry kind of nerves from those awful first few weeks when she'd arrived at the school. This was different – this was nothing but sheer joyous excitement.

The perfect wax-fibre surface along with the thudding rain muffled the sound of Bear's trotting hooves as George circled the arena. Bear was keen, and so was she. His ears were pricked up and she could feel his power as he drove forward with each balanced stride.

All the hard work they'd done together and the proper care she'd given him had made the world of difference to Bear. There was no more rushing from him or snatching at his reins or trying to evade her instructions. They'd practised flatwork to help with Bear's balance. All those transitions from one gait to another, the circles, the serpentines, the figures of eight, the cavalletti pole work to help him pick up his legs that had once felt endless and thankless, now felt like they had all paid off. She was so proud of him.

But it wasn't just Bear who'd improved. George had too in the way she rode him, the way she valued him … the way she loved him.

"Ready when you are, George!" Ms Stopcroft called.

George nodded and moved Bear up into canter as she saw Jessica sitting in the arena seats, watching with a sneer on her face. For once, George didn't mind. She knew that she and Bear were a great team. Jess could sneer all she liked.

Katie, who was in the waiting area with Sheriff, gave George an encouraging smile as they passed, but George's attention was on the course of jumps. She gathered her reins, feeling the supple leather in her gloved fingers. Immediately, Bear responded to her contact and softened even more. How could she ever have doubted him or complained because he wasn't Timmy, ignoring Bear's attempts to be friends: all his gentle nudges and his loving whinnies? George knew he might not be the fanciest horse at Paddock Grove, but Bear tried his heart out for her. He gave it everything he had, and to George, he was as special and as beautiful as Ted.

She turned him onto the long side of the arena, setting up Bear's approach to the first fence. The arena was quiet with anticipation except for the steady sound of Bear's canter – a noise George loved – and once again, she watched his ears point sharply forward, framing the high red-and-white planks of the jump between them.

George maintained the steady, balanced canter, making sure she not only created the correct line with Bear but that she also kept her hands soft. Again, George could feel the power in Bear's hindquarters, and nearing the jump, they took off at the perfect moment, George's body staying in time with Bear's as they launched. A gasp broke out as George smiled – it felt like they were flying through the air! Making sure she wasn't holding the reins too tight so Bear would have the freedom to move his head and neck, they landed superbly balanced with a satisfying thud of Bear's hooves. There was no time to celebrate. George's eyes were up, looking around for the next jump.

They worked together. George didn't need to pull him or try to balance him out any more; they had learnt to read each other beautifully. With her weight anchored firmly down into her heels, George took the tight turn to the huge scopey double down the long side.

Bear responded straight away, gathering himself

for the big challenge. They cantered towards it, and once again Bear's take-off was perfect. For a breathless moment, George wondered if they would hit the pole … but she relaxed quickly as the power of Bear's push-off made it certain they'd clear it.

"George, that was fantastic. Well done – and well done, Bear." Ms Stopcroft's voice rang through the arena. "Glad to see you're living up to your potential. Bear's got great form and a really clean lift when he jumps. All that hard work paid off. You're a good match."

George slowed Bear to a trot. Ms Stopcroft's words meant everything to her. They were more than just an approval of their jumping. George had proved something to herself. She did deserve her place here, however short a time that had been, and she had shown everyone that it wasn't just about the expensive horses and ponies. It was about true partnership.

George leant forward to give Bear a long pat. "You were amazing, Bear."

He turned an ear towards her, and she giggled at him listening as she dismounted and began to walk him towards the arena exit. She couldn't keep the smile from her face, not even when they passed Jessica, who muttered something under her breath. It didn't matter any more. George and Bear had each other.

The pair stepped out into the rain, but George barely noticed the water on her face. She looked up at the grey sky and punched the air with delight, letting out a small whoop of joy. Bear turned his head to watch her.

"Thank you, Bear," she said softly, reaching up to stroke his damp neck. "Thank you for being you."

Chapter Twenty-Two

A BIG SHOCK

All day, the rain continued. George reckoned she hadn't seen so much rainfall in all her life. Some girls had decided not to turn their horses out, and put them on the horse walker instead. Those who didn't want them on the walker had been told by Mr Thatcher that they could put them out in the all-weather turnout pens or the few paddocks at the top near the cross-country course, where the ground drained well and wasn't waterlogged.

George and Lili had decided to put Ted and Bear in the paddocks near the cross-country track. As George stared at the rain becoming even heavier, almost dark, she wished that she hadn't bothered to turn out Bear today. But after the success in the session this morning, she wanted him to be able to stretch his legs and enjoy some grass.

"Does it always rain this heavily here?" George shouted over the rain, which pelted hard on her rain mac as she and Lili splashed their way towards the paddock.

"Always! But this isn't as bad as the island I live on, Lekoala. That has a wet season, and it feels like you're living under a bath tap." She giggled as they quickly hurried up the track to where Ted and Bear were.

George hadn't spoken to Lili about what had happened in the canteen. She hadn't wanted to upset her, and since Lili seemed to be back to her usual self – even talking about life back at home – George didn't want to make her sad again.

As cold droplets trickled down her neck and under her collar, George pulled her jacket tighter, shivering.

"I'm not sure if Bear will be very happy with me, having him out in this," she said.

"At least they've got their turnout rugs on – that's if Bear hasn't pulled Ted's off like he did yesterday."

But as they approached the gate of the all-weather pen, both girls came to a stop. The pen stretched out before them, empty, with not a sign of Ted or Bear anywhere.

"Oh no," George groaned. Thinking Bear must have broken the fence again, her eyes darted around. But the fencing was perfectly intact.

"Do you think this is something to do with Meg again? Look, Ted's head collar has gone," Lili said, staring at the empty gatepost where she always left it. "This is typical of Meg – she's so mean." She frowned, peering through the rain.

"Or perhaps Mr Thatcher has brought them in but took them the other way round and that's why we didn't see them," George said hopefully. She didn't want another run-in with Meg.

"Come on, let's go and see."

"Wait!" George suddenly shouted.

"What is it?" Lili held onto the hood of her coat as the wind got up.

"Look there!" George pointed at a fresh set of tyre tracks cutting deep grooves across the waterlogged grass. They led from the pen and disappeared around the corner where it met the far end of the drive. "They weren't here earlier … and look, there are hoofprints next to them. Two lots!"

Lili stared at George, a look of panic spreading across her face.

"Oh my gosh," George whispered, as her heart began to hammer hard. "The article."

"What article?" Lili answered her, clearly not understanding.

George felt sick. There was no reason for there to be tracks here, next to the hoofprints in the mud … unless… "In the magazine, there was that article about the horse thieves and—"

"And it was right next to the one about how valuable Ted is," Lili finished George's sentence with tears in her eyes. "Someone's taken them, haven't they?" She was visibly shaking.

"But why would they take Bear?" George was crying too now.

"I suppose they couldn't get Ted out of the field without him. He wouldn't go anywhere without his best friend."

George felt her tears mixing with the cold rain on

her face. Bear was gone. Ted was gone. *Stolen.*

"We need to tell Mr Thatcher and Mrs Hawksworth right away," Lili said.

Lili quickly took some photos of the tyre tracks, then they began to make their way back towards the yard. George tried to stop her mind from racing. She didn't want to think about Ted and Bear being with thieves who might be cruel to them. And then there was the guilt – the dark and scary thought that this was an answer to when she first wished Bear away all those weeks ago.

They hurried to Mr Thatcher's office at the stables, but as soon as they told him what they'd seen and showed him Lili's photos of the tracks in the grass, he marched them up to Mrs Hawksworth's office, where George and Lili stood – soaked through and treading mud onto the carpet – as the adults talked about what to do.

"Right," Mrs Hawksworth said. "I'll call the police."

"They could be anywhere by now, though." Lili was shaking. "I can't lose Ted, I just can't."

George nodded miserably, picturing Bear and Ted being driven far away in some horrible horsebox. "The thieves must have been waiting nearby, watching the field. They'll be long gone by now."

Mrs Hawksworth shook her head. "It's been raining too hard. The ford flooded around lunchtime and the road's been closed since."

"And the horses were turned out *after* lunch," Lili said.

Mr Thatcher nodded. "Which means they're still this side of the ford and can't have gone far because there are no other roads out of Paddock Grove."

Mrs Hawksworth looked up at the clock that read 4.15 p.m. "Maybe we still have a chance to bring the boys home. Try not to worry too much. We'll find them, girls."

It was the glimmer of hope George needed to hear.

"Your parents will need to be informed," Mrs Hawksworth said. "Get your housemistress to phone them, then come back to my office. All isn't lost yet… Remember, girls, you have to be at your strongest when you feel at your weakest."

George sighed. Right now, she didn't feel strong at all.

Chapter Twenty-Three

A RETURN

George and Lili sat in dry clothes, huddled together again in Mrs Hawksworth's office. The rain still hammered against the windows, matching their gloomy mood. George had wanted to speak to her parents, even though the housemistress had already spoken to them, and they'd been as upset as she was. Lili had wanted to speak to hers too, but she hadn't told George what they'd said apart from the fact that they'd been asleep. It was the early hours of the morning in Lekoala.

Once more, Mrs Hawksworth assured them that there was no way that a horsebox could have crossed the ford. There was a low bridge cutting off any large vehicles from the main coastal road further to the east, so the only option available to the thieves would be to find somewhere on the Paddock Grove side of the ford to hide the horses and wait for the water level to drop.

She paused, looking at George and Lili. "The police will begin their search in the morning, and if the ford is the only escape, I'm sure they'll guard it."

"In the morning! They can't leave it until then! They have to go and look for them *now*!" George forgot herself and raised her voice.

"Miss Harris, getting worked up won't help the situation. I realize you're worried, as we all are, but the police know what they're doing."

"I'm sorry, Mrs Hawksworth, but they should be searching for them now. It's not even seven o'clock."

"It's far too dark now, and with this rain it's too dangerous to go out looking. As I say, there is no possible way for them to go any further until the flooding subsides, and the police will set up a watch by the ford when it does."

"Bear and Ted will be scared," George blurted out again. "And … and what if the level of the water goes down before anyone predicts and the thieves get away?" She turned to Lili. "Then they'll be gone and that can't happen! We won't ever see Bear or Ted again—"

At that moment, the door to Mrs Hawksworth's office burst open with a bang, making everyone jump. Tabitha stood there, breathless and wide-eyed.

"Quick! Quick!" she shouted. "George, quick."

"Miss Bailey, what is the meaning of this?" Mrs Hawksworth demanded. "You do *not* charge into my office without knocking. Students of Paddock Grove remain composed, no matter what adversity we face."

"But Mrs Hawksworth," Tabitha puffed, gulping in air. "It's Bear! He's back! He's just come trotting down the drive."

George leapt up. "He has? Where is he?"

"Miss Fox has him in the yard."

Lili stood up, hopefully. "Is Ted with him?"

Tabitha's face fell as she shook her head. "No, it's just Bear. I'm sorry."

Mrs Hawksworth stood up too. "This is excellent news about Bear and supports the idea that Ted can't be far from here, and…"

But George was already racing out of the office, too desperate to see Bear to hear any more.

In the yard, Bear was surrounded by a small crowd of the stable staff as Miss Fox checked him over carefully. George pushed through, her heart pounding.

"Bear! Oh *Bear*!" She threw her arms around his wet and muddy neck. "I thought you'd gone. I thought I'd never see you again."

As George stepped back, she noticed something. "That's not his head collar."

Miss Fox nodded. "No, that's one of the school's. He came back without his on." That's when it hit George. She'd forgotten. "The AirTag!" She whirled round to look at Tabitha and Lili, who'd followed her down from Mrs Hawksworth's office. "Lili, remember? You gave me the AirTag and it's still on his field collar."

Lili's eyes widened. "You're right!"

"Maybe he pulled it off and escaped when they were hiding him?"

"Then we could track it!" Lili sounded excited.

"We could go now," George agreed.

"No," Miss Fox said firmly. "It might not be late, but it's dark and the weather's only getting worse. We'll inform the police about the tag and let them handle it."

"But they're not going to start looking until tomorrow!" Lili said despairingly.

"They know what they're doing, Lili. I know it's difficult, but we need to wait until it's light. Why don't you both take Bear and rub him down with some towels and give him some haylage – we don't know when he last ate."

George nodded, relieved that Bear seemed fine. She turned to him. "If only you could tell us where Ted is." Then an idea came to her…

Chapter Twenty-Four

A LATE-NIGHT RIDE

Later that night, George lay awake thinking about Ted being alone. Not only was he with strangers but he was without Bear. She knew he must be terrified. Most of the evening, Lili had been crying, completely inconsolable. The more George thought about it, the more she was certain the thieves only took Bear to persuade Ted to go easily. He wasn't valuable like Ted was. At least that meant Ted would probably be safe – he was worth much more alive and well.

George waited for the housemistress's lights to go out. When there was complete silence apart from the wind and rain battering the windows, she sat up and slipped out from under the covers, creeping over to Lili's bed.

"Lili," she whispered, shaking her friend gently. "Lili, wake up."

"I'm not asleep," Lili whispered through tears. "I can't stop thinking about Ted. He's my best friend and he's gone."

"That's why we need to go and find him," George said firmly.

"What?" Lili sat up.

"I think we should go and look for him. We could start by trying to trace the AirTag."

"But what about what Mrs Hawksworth and Miss Fox said? They wanted us to wait until morning and leave it to the police."

"Is that what you want?" George asked softly. She didn't want to make Lili do anything she didn't want to.

"No..." Lili started to cry again, and George gave her a big hug.

"Oh Lili, we'll find him."

"Do you think so?"

"Yes, but we can't find something unless we go looking," George said.

"I agree with George." Katie's voice broke through

the darkness. She came to sit on Lili's bed and took her hand. "I'm worried about Ted too. The thieves will want to get away from the area as soon as possible."

Tabitha clambered out of bed and came to sit with them.

"I don't want anything to happen to Ted either." She looked anxious. "Last year when the ford was flooded, we couldn't go to the Coastal Region riding competition – we thought we'd miss the whole week – but then overnight the water level went down. It's not as predictable as everyone is making out."

Lili switched on her bedside lamp. She glanced between them all. "So what do we do?"

"I think we should tack up the horses and see if we can find him." George was adamant. She couldn't sit and wait for the morning. She needed to help Lili bring back Ted.

"I'll go and ask Misty if I can take Dream," Lili said. "I'm sure she'll let me. I'll swear her to secrecy, though."

Then they quickly set about changing into their waterproof riding gear as Tabitha heaped clothing under each of their duvets so that, if anyone came to check on them, it would look as if they were still sleeping safely in their beds. Grabbing the torches that were kept in each dorm room in case of a power cut, they rushed along the darkened corridors, riding boots in hand so that they didn't make any noise.

George knew they'd get into terrible trouble if Mrs Winters caught them, but right now, the thought of Ted being taken away by the thieves was all she cared about.

They ran down the stairs of Stroller House, and at Tabitha's suggestion they made their way into the library, unlocking and opening the back window.

"Ready?" George asked as she put on her riding boots, zipping them up.

The others nodded and, one by one, they climbed out of the ground-floor window that overlooked the rose garden.

They ran towards the stables and George looked at Bear. "We're going to find your friend, Bear, and bring him back, and you're going to help us. Will you do that?" She smiled, then hurried into the tack room, punching in the door code to get the saddles.

Fifteen minutes later they were mounted – George

on Bear, Katie on Sheriff and Lili on Dream.

"Are you sure you're fine about waiting here for us?" George asked Tabitha.

It had been Tabitha's idea that she should wait in Bear's stall for them to come back. "Yeah, I think it's best because I can try to cover for you, and if you don't come back, at least I'll be able to tell someone."

"Don't say we won't come back," Katie said, sounding worried.

"I didn't mean it like that, but if anything happens, at least I'll be able to go and get help." She held up her phone. "And you can call me."

"Are you sure about this?" Lili sounded nervous as she sat on Dream, next to Bear.

"It's the only way to get Ted back," George insisted.

Putting on her riding gloves, Lili nodded. "OK, let's go … and thank you, everyone." Lili turned Dream around and headed towards the tracks that would lead them up through the woods to the bridle paths. Katie and George followed, with the sound of the horses' hooves muffled by the rain.

With their torches slotted into the straps on their

hats, they were able to see the track in front of them, although George felt as though the horses knew their way.

The rain lashed at their faces as they rode into the night.

"Let's turn on our phones once we're at the top of the hill," Katie shouted over her shoulder as she guided Sheriff through the trees. George followed on Bear, trailing them nose to tail, the storm howling and the wind feeling like it would rip them from their saddles. Suddenly, a loud crack split the air.

"Look out!" Katie shrieked as a branch snapped overhead. It came crashing to the ground. Sheriff reared up, with wild, fearful eyes. She clung on, leaning forward and wrapping her arms around his neck. Katie's voice was steady and calm. "It's OK, boy, it's alright… That's it… Shh, it's only a branch."

At the same time, Dream skipped sideways, nearly bumping into Bear, who snorted and pawed the ground nervously. But within moments, he was quiet again and true to his unflappable nature.

"Everything OK?" George called out.

"Yep," Katie called back, with Sheriff now under control.

They pressed on, more alert than ever to the dangers of the weather, George pushing away the thought that it had been a really silly idea to come out in the middle of the night to search for Ted.

Rain stung her face as they weaved through the trees and the low-hanging branches. With the woods behind them, they arrived at the top of the hill. Despite the conditions, George could see right across the valley to the coast below. Holding the reins in one hand, she pulled out her phone with the other and opened the tracking app.

She stared at the screen. There was just an endless swirling searching icon. Disappointed, she turned to Lili.

"Nothing."

They rode in silence, with George losing hope with every minute that passed. On the wide, sandy bridle path they carefully picked up the pace, jumping over fallen logs and branches. The only sounds were the horses' hooves, the roar of the wind and the choppy sea in front of them.

After a few minutes, Katie pulled up. "Maybe we should turn back?" she shouted over the storm. "We don't even know if we're going the right way."

George would have loved to be tucked up warmly in her bed. She looked at Katie, hunched miserably in Sheriff's saddle, and Lili trembling as the rain dripped off the peak of her riding hat. But no matter how much she wanted to, they couldn't give up now. Ted needed them.

"Just a little further." George's teeth were chattering with the cold. "We can't let Ted down." Once again, she pulled her phone out of her pocket. It pinged! "I've got something!" she shouted over the wind, continuing to gaze at the screen. "This has to be where Bear escaped from his head collar! Maybe Ted will still be there."

"We're really going to find him!" Lili's voice suddenly sounded determined. "We're going to find Ted!"

The signal was weak, but that didn't matter. All George cared about was the tiny dot blinking. She held out her phone for Katie to have a look as Sheriff executed a dressage-worthy turn on the forehand for her to reach it.

"That's brilliant." Katie grinned as she looked at the phone. "It's not too far away." She pointed towards some trees near the path that led to the beach.

The girls set off again, with George in front holding the phone as she followed the signal.

As they came out of the trees and round a small bend, George saw it. She pulled up Bear and waited for Katie and Lili, who rode up alongside her.

"There." She pointed to an old, weathered barn close to the cliff edge. "The phone's telling me that's where the head collar is." She could barely contain her excitement.

They quickly dismounted, tying their horses to a nearby tree.

"What are we going to do?" Lili whispered.

"I think we should go and look," George said.

"What if someone's there?" Katie sounded worried.

"They won't hear us in the storm," George said with confidence as she stared at the barn. "Besides, I can't see any cars or horseboxes."

"They've probably hidden them somewhere, so no one spots them," Katie said thoughtfully.

"Or maybe they've gone? Let's go and see..."

The girls hurried towards the barn, creeping closer and being careful of the muddy ground.

"Shh." George turned to the others and pressed her eye to a gap in the wooden slats. She gasped. There was Ted! She could just see him in the dim light that was filtering through the shed. Tied up but looking unharmed. His coat wet and muddy. And there on the floor was Bear's field-safety head collar!

"He's in there. I can see Ted," she whispered. "Bear must have broken free like we thought when they tried to tie him up, and as usual he used his escape talents to get out somehow. There's probably an entrance around the front."

"Let me see." Lili couldn't contain herself, and she squeezed in next to George to look through the gaps. "Oh, Ted. Let's get you home," she said quietly.

George squeezed Lili's hand in relief. But before they could make their next move, they heard the sound of an engine. Headlights cut through the darkness as a large horsebox rumbled up the dirt track behind them.

George stared at the lorry. "The thieves are back!"

Chapter Twenty-Five

BREAKOUT

"Quick, hide!" George hissed. "We can't let them see us!"

"What about the horses?" Katie worried, glancing over to the trees where Bear, Dream and Sheriff were tied up.

Lili followed Katie's gaze. "They're well back in the trees – they won't be able to see them from where they are."

The girls ran to the other side of some large rocks clumped by the small, sloping cliff edge and watched as two young men got out of the lorry. George gasped as she saw the height and size of them.

"What are we going to do now?" Katie whispered, her voice wobbling.

"If they take Ted now, I might not ever see him again." Lili began to shake violently and George knew it wasn't just from the cold. Katie wrapped her arms around Lili's shoulders.

"We're going to save Ted," George said firmly. "And we're going to make sure these men *never* steal another horse again." George's voice sounded much more confident than she felt.

"But how?" Katie looked puzzled. George could see that Katie was trying to be brave, but she looked as scared as Lili was, and George instinctively felt it was down to her to do something.

"I need you to distract them," George said, her mind racing. "Get back on the horses, then make some noise and draw them away from the barn. Once they come over to see what's going on, I'll sneak in and get Ted, then ride away back to the school."

Lili stared at her. "We can't leave you."

"I won't be far behind, and I've got my phone. Besides, you said that Ted knew his way back from the beach."

"I don't know, George." Lili gave a weak smile as she stared at the broken-down shack. "It might be dangerous."

"It's the only way to get Ted back. Another twenty minutes and it might be too late." George looked at them both. "I can't think of anything better."

Neither could they. Katie nodded. "OK, but be careful, George. I'll take Bear with me. I'll lead him back with Sheriff."

"I should be doing this, George, not you," Lili insisted. But George could see she was in no fit state to do anything much.

"This is as much my mess as yours. If it wasn't for the disaster at the lunch, you wouldn't have had to do the magazine interview and then no one would've known how much he was worth." She gave Lili a hug. "I can do this, but I need you to do what I've asked."

Before Lili could argue, George ran from behind the rocks to the far side of the barn and ducked down out of sight behind the front of the horsebox. A few minutes later, she heard her friends raising their voices up by the trees. George smiled to herself. Perfect. That's exactly what she'd wanted them to do.

"Hey, what are you doing? Hey you! You there!" one of the men shouted angrily as he came outside. Then,

just as George worried that he'd go and investigate on his own, he leant his head back inside and called for his friend.

"Hey!" both the men called out as they started up towards the trees. "Who's that? Get out of here!"

Hearing their voices, George watched and waited until they headed away. Then she ran inside the barn. A dim light shone out from the ceiling, and the moment Ted saw her, he whickered quietly.

"Shh, boy, it's OK," she murmured, working to untie him. Her fingers were cold, and she fumbled with the knot. "Come on, come on, come on..." She glanced nervously at the barn door.

Finally, the rope gave way, and George looped the loose end of it through Ted's head collar to make a set of reins. "Come on, Ted, let's take you home." She quickly led him out of the barn, murmuring reassurance. "Good boy, we'll get you out of here."

But just then, a shout rang out. "Stop right there!"

The men had seen her. Panic rushed through George as she spotted a torch beam cutting through the darkness and shining towards her.

"Hey you!" they continued to bellow at her. She could hear running footsteps as the torchlight bobbed around.

She began to run, holding onto Ted, then – as she'd done so many times with Timmy when she was leading him to the field – with a quick movement, she grabbed a handful of Ted's mane and swung herself onto his bare back.

"Come on, Ted, go, go! GO!" Scrambling up and ripping him with her legs, she pushed him forward, and he burst into a canter. She was too scared to look behind her. Instead, she concentrated on keeping seated without a saddle on a horse so much taller than her own beloved Bear.

Ted's hooves thundered on the ground but once they were at a safe distance, terrified she might slip off, George slowed to a trot. Through the trees and along the winding path they went, and on the wider, flatter terrain George allowed Ted to explode into canter. It was all she could do to hang on to the makeshift reins of the lead rope, wrapping one hand in Ted's long mane as they cantered along.

Although the rain had calmed down, the wind raged around them. But George could tell that Ted knew exactly where he was going…

Back to Paddock Grove.

Back to home.

Back to Lili.

And after what felt like hours, the school came into view and Ted broke into an eager trot as they approached the yard, which was flooded with light.

"We're here! We did it, Ted… *You* did it." George let out a sob of relief as they clattered into the yard. Her heart did an anxious double time, though, as she saw not only Tabitha and the others who'd made it back safely, but also Mrs Hawksworth and Miss Fox.

"George! Ted!" Lili cried out, running towards them and flinging her arms around Ted's neck. "You made it! Thank you, George, *thank you*."

George slid off Ted's back, her legs aching from tension as they nearly gave way beneath her. Lili reached out to steady her, pulling her into a hug, tears of joy and relief streaming down her face.

"I'm sorry," Tabitha whispered. "I tried to cover for

you, but Mrs Winters came into the dorm and realized we'd all gone."

"All that matters is that Ted is back safely," George whispered back with a grateful smile.

"Miss Harris." Mrs Hawksworth appeared behind them, looking both furious and relieved. "You and your friends went against my *specific* instructions, and while I have no alternative but to find you *all* a suitable punishment…" She paused. "Never let it be said that a true Paddock Grove girl isn't brave in spirit and generous in heart." She reached out and gently stroked Ted. "Well done, Miss Harris."

Chapter Twenty-Six

A DELIGHTFUL SURPRISE

The half term holiday started tomorrow and the autumn sun cast a warm glow over Paddock Grove as George made her way to the stables. The events of the past week felt like a dream, but the sight of Ted happily grazing with Bear in their paddock made George both happy and sad. For all she and Bear had been reunited, in a month or so she'd have to leave the school, her friends and her dreams, and Bear would have to leave Ted.

She sighed loudly, not wanting to think about it any more. At least the thieves had been caught. They'd been picked up two days after she'd rescued Ted. With the police watching the ford, they'd had no hope, and they'd been caught trying to leave town when their lorry had got stuck on the flooded road. The police had even been able to locate the other stolen horses and ponies, and they'd been returned to their owners. There'd also been an article in the newspaper about the thieves, and a journalist had approached the school to interview both George and Lili, but they'd had enough of publicity!

George stroked Bear's neck. "I don't want to leave," she whispered into Bear's mane. He whinnied softly, as if trying to comfort her.

"George! *George!*" Katie suddenly appeared. She panted. "Come and look at this. Quickly, *come on*!"

"What is it?"

"Just come and look," Katie said excitedly.

George followed her, racing through the yard and into the drive, her eyes widening at the sight. A procession of three, four – five! – sleek black cars were winding their way down the drive, led by a motorcycle escort. Students and staff alike were gathering to watch the spectacle.

"What's going on?" George asked Katie.

Katie shrugged, looking just as bewildered. "No idea. But it looks important."

As the cars came to a stop in front of the school,

George spotted Lili standing near the main entrance, fidgeting nervously. Before George could call to her, a chauffeur opened the passenger door of the middle car.

Two elegantly dressed people stepped out.

"Oh my goodness!" George's jaw dropped as she recognized the tall, slim people from the photos on Lili's bedside table in the dorm. "They're Lili's parents!" she whispered to Katie and Tabitha, who were both watching the unfolding scene.

Mrs Hawksworth walked forward, greeting Lili's parents with a deep curtsey.

"Your Majesties," she said, her voice carrying across the suddenly quiet driveway. "Welcome to Paddock Grove."

There was a collective gasp.

"Majesties?" George turned to Katie, who looked just as shocked.

Lili's mother, who had the same warm eyes as Lili and wore an elegant cream suit, smiled. "Thank you for your welcome, Mrs Hawksworth. Thank you for letting us come to express our gratitude to the young lady who saved our daughter's beloved horse."

All eyes turned to George, whose cheeks began to

burn. Lili caught her eye and smiled as her parents made their way towards George.

"Oh my gosh, no way." George heard Meg's shocked voice behind her. "No way is Lili royal! Just wait till I tell everyone I'm friends with royalty!"

George frowned at Meg and shook her head, but she didn't say anything. Friends, indeed!

"This is George." Lili came up and introduced George to her parents.

George wasn't sure what she was supposed to do, and she stepped forward, trying to remember how to curtsey. "Hello," she mumbled. "I … I'm George. Georgia Harris."

"Lili has told us all about what happened." Lili's father smiled kindly. He reached out to shake George's hand. "We can't thank you enough for what you did, and for your bravery. You've not only saved Ted but proved yourself a *true* friend to our daughter."

George blushed, not sure what to say.

Lili's mother stepped forward to kiss George lightly on each cheek. "What you did was extraordinary. And we'd like to repay your kindness."

Mrs Hawksworth hurried towards them, her face serious. "Perhaps we should continue this conversation in my office? May I show you the way? You too, Miss Harris."

Confused, George trailed after Lili and her parents as Mrs Hawksworth led them to the front hallway and up the grand front stairs. It was the first time that George had actually walked up this staircase. She gave Lili a shy smile. What was going on?

"Lili." Her mum turned and smiled at her warmly. "Would you mind waiting outside while we have a talk with Mrs Hawksworth and George?"

Lili looked as puzzled as George felt, but she smiled at her mum. "That's fine," she said, glancing at George again.

Mrs Hawksworth waited for everyone to step into her office before shutting the large oak doors behind her. She walked to her desk and sat behind it, opposite Lili's parents.

"Miss Harris, Miss Nagata's parents have a proposal for you."

Lili's mum looked at her and gave her the same lovely

smile she'd given to Lili. "George. Lili talked about you having to leave the school shortly, and Mrs Hawksworth has told us about what happened with the funding for your scholarship."

George nodded, her chest growing tight as she tried not to cry.

"So, we'd like to continue funding your scholarship, to ensure you can complete your education here at Paddock Grove."

"I–I—What? I—" George couldn't find the words. She glanced at Mrs Hawksworth, then back to Lili's mum. "That's … that's so kind, but I couldn't accept such a big gift."

Lili's dad leant forward, his eyes kind. "It wouldn't just be for you. You've inspired us. We want to establish a long-term scholarship programme, to give other girls the same opportunity that both you and our daughter have."

Mrs Hawksworth nodded. "Their Majesties are proposing to fund a scholarship for one girl in each year group. I spoke to your parents this morning, George, and they're delighted and very happy for you to accept, if that's what you'd like."

George's eyes widened. "Really? That's … that's amazing!" Without thinking, George threw her arms round Lili's mum, giving her a big hug. Mrs Hawksworth looked horrified, but Lili's mum burst into laughter.

"Why don't you go and tell Lili the good news?" she suggested.

"I will. I will … and thank you … *thank you.*" George bubbled with excitement.

"Wait, Miss Harris?" Mrs Hawksworth called her back. She smiled. "It seems I have the pleasure of saying this: welcome *back* to Paddock Grove."

George laughed and burst out of the office. "Lili, Lili, Lili! I'm staying! Your parents are funding the scholarship. I don't have to leave after all!"

Lili – who seemed as shocked at the news as George – squealed with delight, and the girls hugged each other, spinning around on the spot.

"That's brilliant! I'm so pleased, George. Let's go and tell the others…"

As they hurried away from the office, George looked at her friend. It made sense now why Lili had such an expensive horse.

"Why didn't you say anything about your parents?"

Lili shrugged. "I'm sorry I never told you – I never told *anyone*. I just wanted to be treated like everyone else – and people don't tend to do that when they know that you're royalty. That's why I insisted on the DIY livery for Ted, even though my parents wanted me to be on full livery."

George reached out and squeezed her hand. She gave her a wink. "So I don't have to call you Princess Lili?" She burst into laughter and their giggles filled the upper hall.

Katie and Tabitha were waiting together down in the entrance hall, and George charged down the stairs towards them.

"Guess what? *Guess what?*" Tears of joy pricked in George's eyes. "I'm staying… I'm staying. Lili's parents are funding the scholarship."

They all screamed with excitement.

Katie grinned and laughed at the same time. "Oh George, I'm so happy!"

The four friends weren't the only ones waiting in the hall, though. Meg and Jessica were standing by the door.

Meg raised her eyebrows. “Ugh, great, now there’s no getting rid of you, Harris.”

George laughed, but then turned to Lili. “Thank you,” she said softly. “Thank you for everything.”

Lili shook her head. “No, I should be thanking you. For being my friend, for saving Ted.”

George broke away from the group. There was someone else she had to tell…

“I’ll be back in a minute!” She ran out of the main entrance and cut through the side path that took her to the yard, where she raced to Bear’s stable block.

“Bear, guess what? We’re staying! We don’t have to leave.” She stroked his face, and Bear nudged her gently. George roared with laughter as she kissed him on his nose. Her dream hadn’t vanished after all. She had Bear; she had her friends; and she had Paddock Grove.

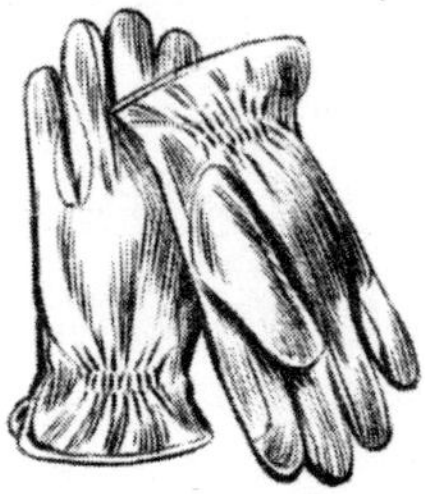

Acknowledgements

What a joy this has been creating and writing this book, but a huge, special thanks has to go to Non Pratt, my editor and fellow pony/horse loving wonderful person. Without Non, this gorgeous book I feel so proud of, wouldn't be out in the world. Non has really made my horsey dreams come true. I also want to thank the rest of Walker Books who have been so wonderfully embracing to me. Then of course, my fantastic agent and friend, Clare Wallace, who is there through thick and thin, and always knows the right thing to say. And without fail a super thank you goes to the rest of the Darley Anderson children's crew who are just a fabulous bunch.

Then thanks to all my family who are my cheerleaders and my joy, always supporting me every step of the way. And to my horsey friends and wonderful riding instructor, the real Ms Stopcroft, Vicki, and of course her dog, Bailey, who has given me the confidence to fly and love every moment of being in the saddle. And not forgetting my wonderful horses who give me so many magical moments that you can't buy.

Lastly, to the readers, I hope that I have created a world where you feel welcome and you feel part of Paddock Grove, a place of dreams, horses and hope. Thank you for reading.

JP

J. P. Rose is an award-winning author whose books for children include *The Haunting of Tyrese Walker* and *Birdie* with Andersen Press. In addition to spending her days surrounded by words, J. P. surrounds herself with her rescue dogs, cats and her magnificent horses. As a child she fell in love with ponies, was an avid rider and dreamed of having her own horse. Now, as an adult, she's lucky enough to have three magical unicorns of her very own, Apache, Boo and Monarch.

MORE ADVENTURES FROM PADDOCK GROVE

Katie – along with her horse Sheriff – intends to lead the Paddock Grove team to victory, but when strange things start to happen around the stables, she suspects that someone is trying to sabotage the school's chances of winning gold…